"
"I KNOW YOU HAVE[...] time you were fiftee[...] you w[...] Alice began. "By th[...] time y[...]

"You're very good." His finger outlined the seductive arch of her upper lip. "Do I want to know how you dug up all that information on me?"

She slowly shook her head. "Trade secret."

His finger slid to her lower lip and tenderly pulled down, so that the tip of his finger traced the moist inner lip. "Did you learn anything about the project I'm working on now?"

"Listed as classified."

He raised an eyebrow at that and leaned in closer. "Really?" He replaced his finger with a fleeting sweep of his tongue. "What else did you find out?"

Desire danced in the wake of his tongue. She could feel his warm breath as it feathered her face. She wanted more. Needed more. Her hungry gaze fastened on his mouth. "Nothing earth-shattering."

"What do you consider earth-shattering, sweet Alice?" he asked, his lips brushing hers.

She'd waited long enough. She pulled him closer and whispered, "Kiss me and I'll show you."

WHAT ARE *LOVESWEPT* ROMANCES?

They are stories of true romance and touching emotion. We believe those two very important ingredients are constants in our highly sensual and very believable stories in the LOVE-SWEPT line. Our goal is to give you, the reader, stories of consistently high quality that may sometimes make you laugh, sometimes make you cry, but are always fresh and creative and contain many delightful surprises within their pages.

Most romance fans read an enormous number of books. Those they truly love, they keep. Others may be traded with friends and soon forgotten. We hope that each LOVESWEPT romance will be a treasure—a "keeper." We will always try to publish

LOVE STORIES YOU'LL NEVER FORGET
BY AUTHORS YOU'LL ALWAYS REMEMBER

The Editors

Loveswept ®715

OUT OF A DREAM

MARCIA EVANICK

BANTAM BOOKS

NEW YORK · TORONTO · LONDON · SYDNEY · AUCKLAND

OUT OF A DREAM

A Bantam Book / November 1994

If you would be interested in receiving protective vinyl covers for your
Loveswept books, please write to this address for information:

Loveswept
Bantam Books
P.O. Box 985
Hicksville, NY 11802

ISBN 0-553-44465-4

Published simultaneously in the United States and Canada

Bantam Books are published by Bantam Books, a division of Bantam Dou-
bleday Dell Publishing Group, Inc. Its trademark, consisting of the words
"Bantam Books" and the portrayal of a rooster, is Registered in U.S.
Patent and Trademark Office and in other countries. Marca Registrada.
Bantam Books, 1540 Broadway, New York, New York 10036.

PRINTED IN THE UNITED STATES OF AMERICA

OPM   0 9 8 7 6 5 4 3 2 1

To Barbara,
Sisters for life.
Love.

ONE

If a spirit shows up tonight, I'll give up coconut cream patties for a month. Alice Jorgensen rolled her eyes heavenward and tried to stifle her irreverent thoughts, along with another yawn, as the medium's heavily accented voice filled the dining room.

"Elmer Jorgensen, show yourself! Give us a sign!" Madame Zeldar's silver bracelets clanged against the wooden table as she swayed back and forth in a trance. "Elmer, your earthbound wife, Maude, is calling you. Show her a sign!"

Alice glanced at her aunt, Maude, who was tightly gripping her hand, and smiled sadly. Every Halloween night for the past fifteen years Maude had tried to contact her deceased husband, Elmer. And every year they received the same results: absolutely nothing. No eerie voices, no floating candles, no mysterious knocks, and no wavering faces of poor, departed souls bobbing across the ceiling.

Alice looked away from her aunt to the fourth person sitting at the dining-room table, besides Madame Zeldar, Aunt Maude, and herself. Uncle Herbert, Maude's brother-in-law, was sound asleep. A light snore tumbled from his slightly parted lips, and the huge black hat he had been wearing had slid down his forehead, shading his eyes from the flickering candles. Herbert's hands still held Madame Zeldar's and one of Alice's white paws.

This year Maude had sent all the way to Gary, Indiana, for the medium. Not only was Madame Zeldar charging Maude a ridiculous amount to summon up poor, departed Elmer, she had also arrived early and had wished to be entertained before performing this séance. No one had had a chance to change out of the costume he or she had worn to pass out candy to the neighborhood children. Uncle Herbert had been the Mad Hatter, Aunt Maude, the Queen of Hearts, and this year Alice had broken tradition and, instead of playing her namesake, had dressed up like the White Rabbit. The heavy fur rabbit suit was uncomfortably warm, the pink makeup covering her nose felt like it was running, and her whiskers were starting to droop. All in all, she was a disgrace to white rabbits everywhere.

Madame Zeldar swayed faster. "Elmer, give us a sign!"

Alice wrinkled her nose as the cloying scent of incense, which Madame Zeldar had lit, penetrated the room. Even if Elmer could contact them, she knew he wouldn't. Elmer never had listened to Maude when he was alive, so why would he do it now?

The grandfather's clock in the front parlor began to bong the hour. Midnight was upon them. The hour in which, Madame Zeldar claimed, the portals into the afterlife opened. Alice fought back another yawn as the second bong vibrated through the old Victorian house.

"Elmer Jorgensen, we implore you. Give us a sign!" cried Madame Zeldar as the sixth bong sounded.

Alice absently rubbed her fur-covered foot against the table leg, trying to scratch an itch. She smiled reassuringly at her aunt and lightly squeezed her trembling hand.

"Elmer, can you hear us?" called Madame Zeldar. "Give us—"

Alice jumped out of her seat and nearly had heart failure as a loud crash sounded in the front parlor. It sounded like a bolt of lightning had struck the front of the house. She ran out of the dining room, past the chiming grandfather's clock in the hall, and into the parlor. Madame Zeldar and Maude were right behind her. Herbert never even stirred.

Alice's fur-covered feet slapped at the hardwood floors and tripped over the fringe of the faded floral rug in the parlor. She slid to a halt and grabbed onto the back of an overstuffed chair as she stared in shock at what lay in the middle of the room. There on the floor between the Carrara marble fireplace and Grandmother Jorgensen's overstuffed horsehair settee was a man. At least she thought it was a man.

He was wearing a silver suit that was sparkling with static electricity. Blue sparks randomly ignited across his body, and the silvery material reflected the orange flames burning inside the fireplace. The silver hood of the jacket was twisted, casting the left side of his face into shadows. A thick lock of brown hair had fallen over his right eye. Alice gaped at the still man. Either he was unconscious or he was dead.

She heard her aunt's shocked gasp behind her and cringed as Madame Zeldar sucked in a deep breath just as the clock finished striking the twelfth bong. Her gaze shifted to the double front doors. Both were still shut tight against the evening's cold. She glanced at the windows, closed and locked. How had their visitor gotten into the parlor, and what had caused that unearthly crash? He surely hadn't appeared out of mid-air. Confused, she glanced up at the plaster ceiling. Not even a crack marked its smooth surface. She cautiously moved around the chair and stood next to the man. The blue sparking had stopped. His complexion appeared pale against the dark shadow of a day's growth of whiskers. She breathed a sigh of relief as she detected the gentle rise and fall of his chest. Whoever he was, he was alive!

Madame Zeldar released her breath in an ear-piercing scream as the man moaned.

Alice and Maude watched as the medium picked up the hem of her multicolored skirt and ran, shrieking, from the house. Her words echoed throughout the peaceful neighborhood. "*I did it! I did it!*" Alice frowned. The neighbors were surely going to love this one. She crossed the room to the front doors and started to close them. For a moment she gazed wishfully out at the dark night, wanting to follow Madame Zeldar. But she couldn't. She had to protect Maude and Herbert from this intruder.

Aunt Maude slowly circled the room and stopped on the other side of the unconscious man. She leaned over as far as her costume would allow and studied the spirit from the other side. With the toe of her red shoe she carefully nudged his arm. A smile lit up her wrinkled face when she connected with a solid mass. "Do you think they're all this good-looking in heaven?"

"Aunt Maude!" Alice exclaimed as she rushed back into the room. "Get away from him." She tried to pull Maude away.

"He's a handsome devil, isn't he?" Maude chuckled. "Do you think he's an angel?"

"More likely a fallen angel," muttered Alice as she surveyed the man's handsome face.

Maude's faded blue eyes gleamed with girlish delight as she examined the skintight silver suit. "He might not be Elmer, but what the heck, I'm keeping him."

"Aunt Maude!" Alice managed to push her aunt away as the man moaned again and tried to open his eyes. She swallowed hard as she ran her gaze over him. Silver boots covered his feet, and the shiny material clung to his long legs, molding to them like a second skin. Her gaze slipped up his thighs to the thick bulge nestled between them. A heated flush swept over her cheeks as she forced her gaze upward to a broad chest, wide shoulders, and muscular arms. Spirit from the beyond, fallen angel, space alien, or man—whoever he was, he was sure impressive-looking. The sound of crinkling material drew her gaze to his hands. They were gloved in the same shiny material as the rest of his body, and they were moving. Her glance flew up to his face. He was coming around.

Alice and Maude instinctively stepped back from him. Maude's hands fluttered against her chest as Alice reached behind her, gripped the iron poker, and raised it above her head.

Dr. Clayton Williams groaned and slowly opened his eyes. Everything was a blur. He raised his hand to his face, searching for his glasses. They weren't there. He rubbed his eyes and tried to focus on a shiny object on the other side of the room. A moment later he identified the object as a lit kerosene lamp adorned with dozens of crystal pendants. He rubbed his eyes again. That couldn't be!

Cautiously he turned his head and encountered the curious gaze of an elderly woman. At least he thought it was a woman. Tufts of gray curls stuck out from under a red heart-shaped bonnet, and she appeared to be wearing some type of wooden dress with hearts painted all over it. He blinked rapidly when she smiled, or at least he thought it was a smile. It looked more like a gesture of intent—wicked, lustful intent. Clayton hurriedly glanced away from that possessive gleam and studied his surroundings with a sinking heart.

A red overstuffed settee sat next to him, and two fat armchairs were near the velvet-draped windows. The only light in the room came from the kerosene lamp and the fireplace. Trinkets and knickknacks covered every conceivable space, and the walls seemed to groan under the strain of dozens of paintings. The only thing that outnumbered the lace doilies that were everywhere was the plants. It looked as if dozens of tree-size plants, medium-size bushes, and miniature ferns were crowded into the room. One thing was for sure. Wherever he was, he wouldn't die from lack of oxygen.

He slowly sat up and shook his head one last time, hoping to clear the images. It didn't work. He was still sitting on the floral carpet in what appeared to be a Victorian parlor, circa the late eighteen hundreds.

The teleportation machine had screwed up royally. Not only had he traveled through space, he had traveled through time as well!

He took inventory of his body and breathed a sigh of relief. He appeared to be in one piece. Clayton wiggled his toes just to be sure, and caught a movement out of the corner of his eye. Turning his head toward the fireplace, he froze. There, less than a yard away from him, was a foot. A big, furry white foot. His gaze slowly traveled up the creature's furry legs, across its body, and rested on its face. He expected to see more fur and razor-sharp teeth. Instead a clean-shaven, pink-nosed, floppy-eared rabbit stared down at him with the biggest blue eyes he had ever seen. The mutant bunny looked scared to death, as if someone had pinned it in the headlights of an oncoming car. His gaze traveled up its arms to the fire poker clutched in its paws. Maybe it wasn't fear he had read in the rabbit's eyes. Maybe it was hostility.

Clayton scooted back away from the creature and felt the settee dig into his back. What in the hell was he going to do now? He hadn't just traveled through time and space; he had landed in another dimension!

The rabbit raised the poker higher and in a shaking, feminine voice asked, "Who are you?"

Clayton blinked in surprise. "You speak English!"

"Of course I do." She waved the poker threateningly. "Answer the question. Who are you and how did you get in?"

He rubbed the back of his head where a small lump was forming. His landing hadn't been as smooth as he would have liked. "Can I at least get off the floor first?" With the help of the settee he pulled himself up and plopped onto the overstuffed piece of furniture.

"Don't try anything funny, mister," the rabbit said. "I'm not afraid to use this." She waved the poker again.

"Put that away, Alice," the elderly woman exclaimed. She reached for a red satin pillow with gold fringe and an embroidered picture of Niagara Falls on it, fluffing it before passing it to her visitor. "Here, put this behind your head and rest. You must be exhausted from your trip."

"Ah, thanks." Clayton took the pillow and frowned at the picture. What in the hell was Niagara Falls doing in another dimension?

The rabbit—who apparently was called Alice—stepped nearer and lowered the poker a few inches. "Cut that out, Maude. He could be dangerous."

"Nonsense, dear." Maude straightened the doily he had wrinkled when he'd sat on the settee. "You're just jealous because he's mine."

Clayton glanced between the two creatures. There

obviously was some tribal ritual as to who got the guest. He noticed a tide of red sweep up the rabbit's face. Whoever heard of a blushing bunny?

"He's not yours, Maude." She stepped closer and gently nudged his leg with the poker. "He's no more a spirit than you and I are."

"But Madame Zeldar made him appear for me." Maude placed her hands on her ample hips through the slits of the wooden dress and glared at the rabbit, then turned a wide, inviting smile on Clayton. "Are you a spirit from the beyond?"

"Beyond what?"

Her smile faded a couple of watts. "From beyond the grave. You know, heaven, pearly gates, streets paved with gold. You know." She waved her arms in the air. "The afterlife."

Clayton's mouth fell open in astonishment as he jumped to his feet. His vision was clearing and his mind had started taking in some more of his surroundings. "You think I'm a ghost!" He walked over to the mantel and examined two pictures in silver frames. One was of a middle-aged couple standing in front of a split-level house. The man was dressed in a green leisure suit and the woman wore a flowery dress that ended above her knees. The other picture was of an elderly couple sitting on an old-fashioned porch swing. Neither was dressed in Victorian-style clothes. Confused, he glanced out into the main hallway. Something about the lighting bothered him.

"If you aren't a ghost, who are you?" Alice raised the poker again and followed him into the hall.

Clayton gazed up at the hall ceiling light. It was electric! He glanced around the hallway and frowned. Orange and black crepe paper decorated the wooden spindles and banister on the stairway. A life-size skeleton hung by a nearly invisible thread over a hot-air vent, causing it to wiggle in the air current. A ghoulish face was painted onto a mirror, and a jack-o'-lantern was sitting on a small table alongside a big bowl with a few candy bars in it. Comprehension finally dawned. He spun around and grinned. "It's Halloween!"

"Of course it's Halloween." Alice glanced at his silver suit. "Why else would you be dressed like that?"

He pointed a finger at the elderly woman. "You're the Queen of Hearts." His finger moved to Alice. "And you're the White Rabbit."

"Well, give the man a kewpie doll," Alice drawled sarcastically. "And *who* might you be?"

Clayton headed for another archway without answering. He stepped into the candlelit dining room and studied the elderly man sitting at the table sound asleep. A light snore penetrated the room. Noticing the large black hat and formal short-waisted coat, Clayton said, "Let me guess. He's the Mad Hatter."

"Wrong, he's my uncle, Herbert." Alice tapped him on the chest with the poker. "I want some answers, bub, and I want them now."

Clayton spied a newspaper lying on a sideboard and dashed over to it. He was pretty sure he was in America and about the same time as he had left, but he wanted some more answers before he started to volunteer any of his own. His hostesses would probably find it weird if he asked what year it was. He picked up the newspaper, held it close to his face, and squinted. A wide grin spread across his face. Not only was it dated the date he'd agreed to step into the teleportation machine, but it was the local newspaper of the same town in which the university was located. He just needed to know how far off his landing had been. "Where's Harper University?" he asked Alice.

She pointed. "The campus starts about two blocks over."

Clayton dropped the newspaper, grabbed the startled-looking rabbit, and spun her around in a circle. His laughter caused Herbert to snort twice before finding a more comfortable position and falling back to sleep. The experiment worked! He had traveled through space. Granted the landing was off, and he had misplaced his glasses, but it was an unconditional success for the first test run. Granted he was supposed to have landed in the sealed-off gymnasium on the campus, not in someone's house. Now that he thought about it, he should be counting his lucky stars he hadn't landed in the burning fireplace or been shot as an intruder.

"Put me down!" Alice cried.

Clayton stopped spinning the furry rabbit. His grin faded as he realized that there was indeed a woman underneath all that fur. He could feel the curves of her breasts against his palms. He slowly lowered his hands and encountered the gentle flaring of her hips before he released her completely. His curious gaze fastened on her face. Now that she was standing mere inches away, he couldn't fathom how he had mistaken her for some alien creature. Eyes the color of the morning sky gazed up at him. He couldn't see what color her hair was because it was under the hood of her costume, but judging by the light color of her eyebrows, he would wager it was golden blond. Her complexion was flawless, except for the smearing of pink across her nose, and her generous mouth was pouting seductively. He stared at that tempting mouth and wondered what a person wore under a white furry costume.

Clayton rubbed his eyes again and wished for the twelfth time that he hadn't lost his glasses during the transport. The team should have let him wear his contacts like he'd wanted to. At least then he would have been able to see properly and wouldn't be imagining that Alice, the white rabbit, was actually sexy. Maybe he had clunked his head harder than he had thought.

Embarrassed by his thoughts, he hastily took a step back and muttered something about her nose being smeared.

Alice instinctively raised her hand and muttered a curse at the furry paw there instead of her hand. She jammed her fists onto her hips and stomped her right foot. "All right, bub, the game isn't funny any longer. Who are you?"

"Alice!" Maude said. "Where are your manners?" She turned toward their guest and sweetly asked, "Would you care for a cup of tea? I have some fresh-baked pumpkin cookies in the kitchen."

The silver-suited stranger turned to Maude and smiled warmly at her. "Thank you, but no." As Maude's own smile faded, he added, "Perhaps some other time."

He turned to Alice, still tapping her foot. "My name is Clayton Williams and I work at the university."

"*Doctor* Clayton Williams?" she asked in awe. Her foot stopped tapping.

"You know me?"

"I've never met you, but I've heard about you." She would had to have been living in a cave not to have heard about the gorgeous doctor who'd joined a select team of research scientists two months earlier at the university. Rumor had it he was handsome as sin, always had his nose in some book, and had the unflattering tendency of ignoring every female member of the university's staff who tried to gain his attention. "I'm Alice Jorgensen, and this is my aunt, Maude Jorgensen." She glanced at the man still sleeping on a dining-room chair. "I believe you have already met my uncle, Herbert." She pulled off her furry paws and held out her hand. "I work at the university's library."

"Nonsense, Alice." Maude bumped her niece forward another step closer to Clayton. "She doesn't just work there, she runs the place. She's the chief information specialist."

One of Clayton's dark brows shot up as he took her hand. "You're A.J. aren't you? You did some fantastic research on Einstein's relativity of time for me last week."

"Yes, and you sent over a note thanking me." She had spent hours of her own time gathering the information he had requested. Granted it had been a fascinating subject and she really hadn't minded doing it, but receiving something more rewarding than a wrinkled napkin from the local pizza shop with "A.J.—excellent work! C.W." scribbled on its back would have been nice. A polite phone call would have made her day.

He looked abashed. "I meant to call you the next day and thank you properly, but it must have slipped my mind." He smiled boyishly and squeezed her fingers. "Forgive me?"

"Of course." She released his hand and tried to ignore that devastating smile. Women's hearts had been known to break over lesser smiles. "Can I ask you a question?"

"Anything."

"How did you get into our parlor?" She had to agree with the rumors about how handsome he was—that is, if he would stop squinting at everything. But it was the other rumors that were causing her some concern. The gossip spreading across campus was that Dr. Williams and the five other highly respected scientists were working on a secret project for the government. Words like *time travel, teleportation,* and a possible fifth dimension had been whispered about. Not for a moment would she believe such a thing—it sounded like some outdated science fiction movie—but she was very curious as to how he'd happened to become unconscious in her parlor.

He ran his fingers through his uncombed hair and nervously shifted his weight from foot to foot. "The front parlor, you say . . ." He rubbed at the light growth of whiskers covering his jaw and refused to meet her gaze.

Alice knew a stall when she saw one. Dr. Clayton Williams wasn't going to reveal anything to her or Aunt

Maude. She had a sinking feeling that they might be better off not knowing.

He was saved from answering her question anyway by the chiming of the doorbell. She heard his sigh of relief as he followed her down the hall toward the double doors. "Are you expecting anyone at this hour?" he asked.

She smiled serenely as she reached for the knobs. "It's just one of those nights. People seem to be dropping in unannounced." She opened the doors and cringed at the sight of Madame Zeldar and two police officers standing on her porch.

"Alice Jorgensen?" asked one of the officers.

"Yes, I'm Alice." She opened the screen door. "Won't you come in." She waved at her aunt. "This is Maude Jorgensen, my aunt, and this"—her hand fluttered in Clayton's direction—"is Dr. Williams from the university."

"He is not," cried Madame Zeldar, who hadn't entered the house. She pointed a red-tipped finger at Clayton. "He's Elmer Jorgensen, Maude's dead husband."

The two police officers shared a pained look before glancing back at Madame Zeldar. "He doesn't look dead to us, ma'am."

"That's because I'm not," Clayton said. "What is going on here?"

"I think I can explain," Alice said. She had noticed the cautious look that had entered Clayton's eyes. She didn't even want to fathom a guess as to how he came to be in their parlor, but her loyalty to the university urged her to help him out. "Every year my aunt hires a medium to perform a séance to try to contact her departed husband, Elmer." Alice smiled at the pallid medium, who had finally joined the others in the hallway. "This year she hired Madame Zeldar."

The medium nodded her head in confirmation as the police officers glanced her way. "We were right in the middle of the séance," continued Alice, "when Dr. Williams came to call. He had contacted me earlier about a room we have for rent, and we agreed he could stop by tonight to see if it was suitable." Alice flashed a smile at Clayton. "I guess we were so caught up in the séance that we didn't hear him knocking. Knowing that I was expecting him, he just came in."

Clayton nodded and managed to look sheepish. "I tried to be quiet so as to not to disturb them, but I tripped over the fringe on the rug in the parlor. I must have bumped my head and blacked out." He rubbed the back of his head.

"We heard the crash," Alice went on, "and found him lying on the parlor floor. Before I could explain to Madame Zeldar who he was, she ran from the house screaming something about spirits." Alice smiled apologetically at the medium. "I'm sorry for your fright, Madame Zeldar, but as you can see, Dr. Williams isn't one of the spirits from the beyond."

"I know a spirit when I see one," exclaimed the medium. She moved closer to the two officers and pointed a trembling finger at Clayton. "And you are a spirit."

Clayton sighed and shared a concerned look with the two officers. One of them tried to put Madame Zeldar's fear to rest. "If you aren't a spirit," he asked Clayton, "why are you dressed like that?"

Clayton glanced at his silvery suit, then at the lit pumpkin with its silly smile sitting on the table. "It's Halloween."

"Yeah, but what are you supposed to be? Aren't you a little old to go trick-or-treating?"

Alice read the confusion clouding Clayton's expression and helped him out. "He just left a faculty Halloween party." She picked up the large bowl, still half full of candy bars, and offered the police officers one. "I'm afraid his hat got smashed during his fall, but I'm sure you would have recognized the Tin Man from *The Wizard of Oz* if he had it on."

Clayton grabbed a candy bar and tore the wrapper with his teeth. "Would you believe someone swiped my plastic ax at the faculty party too?" He took a huge bite of caramel-coated peanuts and chocolate and grinned at the officers.

The officers turned to Alice and her aunt. "We are sorry for the disturbance, ma'am. But we had to investigate the complaint."

"I understand completely," Alice said. "I can understand how Madame Zeldar might have jumped to the wrong conclusion."

"I know what I saw!" Madame Zeldar said. "He came from the heavens. Flashing lights were dancing across his body."

Alice shook her head. "It was only the reflection of the flames from the fireplace on his shiny costume."

"I know what he is!" cried the medium as the officers

escorted her back out the door and onto the front porch. "He's a messenger from heaven. He's here to warn us!"

Alice worried her lower lip as the two officer guided the raving woman down the walk and into the back of the patrol car. As they went, she heard one ask Madame Zeldar if she had any family they could contact. As the car pulled away from the curb, Alice closed the door and leaned her forehead against the cool wood. *What had she done?* She had willingly and knowingly lied to the police. She turned her head and gazed at Dr. Williams. The frightening part was she had done all that for a man she didn't know.

"I owe you a very big thank-you," he said as he bowed slightly.

Alice mustered a fragile smile. "Send me a note."

He chuckled. "I'll try to make sure this time it won't have any tomato sauce on it."

"You do that." She moved closer to her aunt, who was looking rather confused by everything. "I think it's time we woke up Herbert and sent him to bed, Auntie."

"Oh my, yes," Maude said. "You know how he gets if he doesn't get his proper rest."

"I think I'd better be going too," Clayton said. "Thanks again, Alice." He turned to Maude. "Thanks for letting me visit, Maude."

"Oh, anytime, young man." She waved cheerfully. "You drop in anytime."

Clayton grinned as he stepped onto the porch. "Next time I'll knock harder." He turned back to Alice. "I'll be seeing you."

"Good-bye, Dr. Williams," she said.

"It's Clayton, Alice." He stepped off the porch and read the wooden sign by the walkway. JORGENSEN'S BOARDING HOUSE, CLEAN ROOMS AND HOME COOKING. He turned back toward the house. "Oh, Alice, one more thing."

"What's that?"

"You look adorable as a bunny." He chuckled softly as he strode down the walkway and headed for the university.

Alice wrinkled her nose and closed the door. She had no idea if she had done the right thing by lying to the police. The only logical explanation for how Dr. Williams had ended up in her front parlor was beyond belief. No one could travel through space that way. Not even the whiz-kid scientist from M.I.T.

She shook her head and turned off the porch lights. "Come on, Maude, bedtime."

"Is the nice doctor taking the room?"

Alice smiled fondly at her aunt. The years were piling up rapidly for Maude and Herbert. They both had been there for her when she needed them, when she'd been left without a mother or father at the age of thirteen, fifteen years ago, when her parents were killed during an expedition in the Amazon. The newly widowed Maude and bachelor Herbert had opened their hearts and home to a heartbroken child and healed her pain with love and kindness. Now, as her aunt and uncle were getting on in years, it was time for Alice to return the gift. She placed her arm around her aunt's shoulders and squeezed. "I don't think so, Maude. He said he'd let me know tomorrow."

"Wouldn't it be wonderful, though!" Maude said excitedly. "Having a real doctor living here." She rearranged the candy bowl next to the jack-o'-lantern. "We never had a doctor living here before. I remember once we had a mortician for a month. Horrible little man. Never smiled and always wore black." Maude rambled on as she headed for the dining room.

Alice leaned over and blew out the candle that was still burning in the jack-o'-lantern. There didn't seem any reason to try to straighten Maude out on Clayton's title of doctor. The chances of Maude seeing the doctor again were as great as another scientist appearing out of thin air in their parlor.

TWO

Alice reached around her aunt and swiped a piece of Italian bread. She dipped it in the sauce bubbling away on the back burner and took a bite. "Explain the phone call again, Aunt Maude. I think you must have gotten something confused."

"I didn't get anything confused," Maude said defensively. "The nice young doctor said he would be here around six, and I said I would hold dinner for him."

"Are you sure it was Dr. Williams from last night?"

"Of course I'm sure," Maude huffed. "How many doctors do you think I know?" She lightly tapped Alice's fingers with the wooden spoon she was using to stir the noodles. "Don't pick. You won't eat your dinner."

"Well, it's six-fifteen and I'm starving." Alice tried to swipe another slice of bread and failed. She had no idea why Dr. Williams would call to say he was coming over. Maybe Maude's forgetfulness was getting a lot worse. She hugged her aunt and placed a kiss on her wrinkled brow. "I'll wait a couple more minutes before I start to nibble on the good china."

Maude chuckled and gently pushed her away. "You get more and more like your uncle Elmer every day." She tasted the sauce. "He had a wicked sense of humor too."

Alice noticed a distinct tear in her aunt's eye. Last night's séance had obviously brought back some fond memories. She lovingly squeezed Maude's hand as the doorbell chimed. "You finish cooking while I go see who that is."

Maude beamed. "It's the doctor, silly. Remember, I told you he was coming." She pulled one noodle from the boiling water and tasted it.

Alice walked down the hall, heading for the front doors. She guessed she'd have to call Dr. Williams later and see why he had phoned. That is, *if* he had phoned. She opened the doors and stared in surprise at Dr. Williams standing on the front porch. One shocked word tumbled from her lips. "You!"

He didn't speak for a moment as his gaze traveled over her, from the red socks covering her feet to the surprised look in her eyes. "Who else were you expecting?" he asked. "Tweedledum and Tweedledee?" He picked up one of the suitcases standing on the porch beside him.

Alice stared in horror at the mound of suitcases. "Maude mentioned something about you renting the Captain's Room."

"And you didn't believe her?" He reached for another suitcase.

She automatically started to help him with the luggage. "Maude has a tendency to confuse things." She frowned at the two brown suitcases in her hands. "Are you really going to be staying here? What happened to where you were staying?"

"The motel?"

She frowned. "The university didn't find you a house?"

"I asked them not to." He shouldered the door open farther and deposited the bags in the hall near the bottom of the stairs. "A house would be too big for just me." He looked a little sheepish. "And I have a tendency to misplace things. In a house it could take me weeks to find anything. I was going to look for a small apartment after I got here, but I never got around to it."

Alice set the suitcases she was carrying next to the other ones. "But this is a boardinghouse, not apartments."

"I know, and it's perfect. I will only have one room to lose things in, and Maude explained that for a small fee I could join the family for meals."

Over the years there had been plenty of guests who had joined them for meals, but for some reason the thought of Clayton joining them disturbed her. "What about your privacy?" Gorgeous hunks needed their privacy, didn't they? Today Clayton wasn't squinting and she could see the color of his eyes. They were green, no, they were hazel. Sexy as sin, golden-flecked hazel.

"What about my privacy?" Clayton returned to the porch for the last two bags. "The university highly recommended this place." He set them on the bottom step.

"I was told that Maude's had many visiting professors and university guests stay here over the past fifteen years." He cocked one brow. "Is there a problem with me staying here?"

"Ah, no." Alice tried to gather her scattering thoughts. To encounter the gorgeous scientist in the hallway every morning for the next couple of months would be difficult enough. To pleasantly wish him good night in that same hallway would be pushing the limits of her endurance. She was only human, after all. The man had caused her hours of sleeplessness the night before, and when she had finally fallen asleep, he had taken over her dreams in a most embarrassing way. "It's just that you might be more comfortable in your own apartment."

He glanced around the hallway, still decorated for Halloween, and smiled. "If I lived in an apartment, I would either have to eat out every meal or chance dying of ptomaine poisoning."

"You should learn to cook." Why was she trying to talk him out of staying there? Maude's income for the past fifteen years, since her husband had died, had come from renting out rooms and from a meager Social Security check every month.

Clayton grinned. "I made a pot of coffee once when I was doing graduate work at M.I.T."

"What happened?"

"Six of us spent the day in the infirmary, and the two lab assistants who were tea drinkers used the rest of the pot as substitute rocket fuel." He chuckled softly. "If I could ever duplicate that mixture, I could retire a millionaire."

Alice shuddered and glanced at the eight mismatched suitcases sitting near her feet. It looked like Maude had a new boarder, and there wasn't a whole lot she could do about it. The only objection she had to Clayton was his looks and his inappropriate behavior in her dreams last night. Two things the poor man had no control over. She could handle Dr. Hazel Eyes as long as he could stand Maude's mothering and Uncle Herbert's habit of napping everywhere. "We have one very strict rule here."

"What's that?"

A teasing smile played across her mouth. "No guests are allowed to make the coffee."

Maude stepped into the hallway and smiled at the laughing couple. "Dinner's ready."

Clayton reached for the bowl of meatballs for the third time. "Honestly, Maude, I haven't tasted spaghetti this good since . . ." He heaped four meatballs onto a small mound of noodles. "Since never." He grinned wickedly at the older woman. "How many beaux am I going to have to fight my way through every night just to eat your cooking?"

Maude flushed a delicate pink and fussed with her napkin. "I'm too old for a beau."

"Oh, yeah?" Alice grinned. It had been a long time since she'd seen her aunt get all flustered. "If that's so, why do I keep tripping over George Ingels around here?"

"Professor Ingels, our neighbor?" Maude asked. "He and I share a love of flowers and plants, that's all."

Alice shared an amused glance with Herbert. "What do you think, Herbie? Does George have the hots for Maude or what?"

"Really, Alice!" Maude exclaimed.

"Just because I had to replace the hinges on the side yard gate twice since George retired doesn't mean a thing, Alice," Herbert said. He tried to cover his laughter with a napkin as he stood up. "Excellent meal, Maude, excellent." He patted his ample stomach.

"Aren't you staying for dessert?" Maude asked. "I baked two apple pies this morning."

"I've got to digest that second helping of spaghetti first." He pushed in his chair and yawned. "Perhaps after a little nap there will be room." He walked out of the room and headed for the nearest napping place, the well-worn couch in the family room where all the cushions had been broken in by him years ago.

Clayton finished the last noodle on his plate and groaned. "I have to agree with your brother, Maude. I need to digest that *third* helping before I could start in on your pie."

"Herbert was my husband's brother," Maude said. "He's the last of the Jorgensen brothers." She rose and began to clear off the table. Alice and Clayton immediately started to help.

"I understand your husband passed away years ago,

Maude." Clayton picked up the bowl of remaining meatballs. "I'm sorry."

"Don't be. He died doing what he loved."

"That was?" He followed her into the spacious kitchen at the back of the house and placed the bowl on a counter.

"He had a dangerous hobby. He was a Barnstormer." Maude gazed out the window above the sink and studied the darkness. "He was performing a barrel roll with his Sopwith Camel down in Harrison County during an antique air show." She shuddered and quickly rinsed off a plate. "The engine stalled."

Clayton shared a concerned look with Alice. "I'm sorry, Maude."

"Don't be. It happened a long time ago." She wiped her wet hands on a towel and headed back into the dining room.

Clayton watched her leave and turned to Alice. "I didn't mean to upset her."

"You didn't." Alice dumped the meatballs into a plastic container and sealed the top. "Maude knew the risks when she married Elmer."

"That he could be killed doing barnstorming?"

"No, that he was a Jorgensen. The Jorgensen brothers were dreamers. They were always reaching for the impossible, taking chances, pushing the edge."

"How many brothers were there?"

"Six." Alice rinsed off the plates she had carried in and started to load the dishwasher. "Herbert is the only one alive and that's only because he stopped dreaming a half century ago."

"Why did he stop dreaming?" Clayton handed her a bunch of silverware.

"He was an army captain stationed in France during World War Two and fell in love with a woman there. Herbert's dream was of medals of honor, ticker-tape parades, and five shiny stars attached to his collar. He took his men out on a daring mission one day. When they returned to the village they were supposed to protect, they found it in ashes. The Nazis had entered the town, killing half its residents, including the woman he loved. Herbert stopped dreaming that day."

"That's terrible."

"War is full of terrible stories." She closed the dishwasher and rinsed off her hands. "I'll go check and make sure Maude has everything ready for you."

Clayton leaned against the counter and watched the enticing view as she left the room. Tight, faded jeans molded long legs, and the baggy red Harper's University sweatshirt dipped and curved in all the right places. Last night he'd suspected that underneath that rabbit suit was a beautiful woman. He just hadn't known how beautiful. Now that he had his contacts in and she wasn't dressed as a rabbit, he could see clearly what had been nothing but a white blur to him the night before. His guess about her hair color had been right on the money. Alice's hair was as golden as the morning sun and fell all the way down to the middle of her back. His fingers had trembled throughout dinner with the need to sink themselves into the silky mass.

He had also noticed over dinner that Alice didn't use any makeup, and the only fragrance he could detect was a light herbal scent that was probably her shampoo. Her small hands looked capable of strength or of great tenderness. The nails were trimmed short, and they weren't painted. Alice Jorgensen was certainly different from most women he knew.

She had even tried to talk him out of staying there. Why? The dean's secretary at the university had been quite adamant that Maude's was the best boardinghouse in town. She had assured him that the rooms were large and clean, and the meals were plentiful and excellent. Many returning guests had insisted on staying there again. Clayton hadn't needed any convincing, he had just been curious about the Jorgensens. Maude obviously hadn't understood everything that had happened last night, but Alice had a pretty good idea what was going on. He had seen it in her eyes. She'd had plenty of opportunity to spill the beans, but she had remained silent. She had even gone so far as to lie to the police for him. Why?

Even as he'd packed and left the motel, he hadn't understood his strong desire to move in with the Jorgensens. He had been on his own for years, living only for his work, but something about Alice and her family compelled him. Was it the way Alice protected her aunt that drew him in? Or was it some deep, hidden need to belong, to become part of a family once again?

He was dying to ask about her parents. Her father obviously had been one of the daring Jorgensen brothers who had lost his life. That was something else they had in common. He had lost both of his parents when he was sixteen. Alice had an aunt and uncle to comfort her through her loss. He had been blessed with a grandmother who had loved and supported him until her death, two short years after his parents'. He wondered what dream Alice's father had followed, and what had happened to her mother. More unanswered questions.

Alice was provoking too many whys. He hated unanswered questions. He had to deal with them every day in his work; he wasn't about to put up with them during his time away from the lab. He pushed away from the counter and headed for his room and the sexy woman who had tantalized his dreams last night.

There was something intimate in the simple act of making a bed. Alice smoothed the pale-blue sheets Clayton would be lying on that night and fluffed both pillows on the double bed. A big, lonely double bed, just like the one down the hall where she slept. *Dangerous thoughts, Alice!* She frowned at the bed and jerked up the hand-stitched quilt. Now she couldn't even make up a bed without thinking about what he would look like lying naked beneath the sheets. Cripes, if she was this bad now, when his luggage wasn't even in the room, what would she be like in a week?

She turned away from the bed and halted at the sight of Clayton leaning against the doorjamb watching her. "Oh, I didn't hear you come up." She willed the tide of red threatening to flood her face to disappear.

"That's because you were humming 'The Battle Hymn of the Republic.'" He stepped into the large room and placed the two suitcases he had carried up with him down near the bed. Looking around, he gave a low whistle. "I can see now why this is called the Captain's Room." The room was done in massive dark-wood furniture and deep blue. The same color blue the Union soldiers had worn during the Civil War. Pictures from the Civil War hung from every wall.

Clayton studied a silver-framed photograph next to the sturdy oak dresser. "Isn't that Grant?"

Alice walked over to him and pointed at each man standing rigidly in the photograph. "That's Grant, that's Sherman, Burnside, and this is my great-great-grandfather, Captain Jedidiah Jorgensen."

"Shouldn't these photos be in a museum or something?" He slowly walked around the room and studied each photo.

"The family donated over half of Jedidiah's collection of Civil War memorabilia years ago." As she spoke, Alice realized this room could no longer be called the Captain's Room. Clayton had claimed it as his own just by walking in, and his presence in the room was overpowering. She could detect the faint fragrance of his aftershave. It was spicy and cool, the perfect combination to drive a woman crazy. She needed to get out of his bedroom.

She checked the adjoining bathroom to make sure there were plenty of towels and soap, then gave the room one last glance. "I hope you find the room comfortable. The only rooms in the house that are off-limits to the guests are the family's bedrooms and baths. You may have the complete freedom of the first floor." She studied the pattern on the area rug as she slowly backed out of the room. "If you need anything, just let Aunt Maude or myself know."

"There is one thing, Alice."

She reluctantly raised her gaze to his. "What?"

A smile teased the corner of his mouth. "Thank you."

"For what?"

"For recommending this place. It wasn't until last night when you told the police I was here about a room that it dawned on me what a wonderful concept a boardinghouse was."

"I didn't recommend it to you," Alice snapped. She immediately softened her voice. "It was just a spur-of-the-moment fib." There was no way she was taking the blame for him staying there. She would have preferred him at the Holiday Inn out on Route 83, in a dormitory, or even setting up house in the abandoned mansion up on top of No Man's Mountain. Anywhere but under the same roof with her and her family. They had had their share of dreamers to last a lifetime.

"As it turns out," he said, "it wasn't a fib after all."

"Is that why you're here?" she asked. "Are you afraid the police will come back to see if you rented a room?"

"No, I'm here because I'm sick of sterile motel rooms, coffee out of Styrofoam cups, and pizza five nights a week." He chuckled to lighten his words. "Besides, I heard Maude is the best cook in three counties."

Her heart gave a strange lurch as the meaning of his words became clear. "If you continue to eat every meal with as much zest as tonight's, I'm afraid Maude is going to have to increase your rent."

"It would be worth it." He followed her down the steps and picked up the remaining suitcases. "How are her pies?"

"Why don't you go unpack first and make some room for them?" Maybe she had misjudged Clayton after all. He might be a dreamer, but he was obviously lonely. "The last time George Ingels stayed for dessert, he ate half a pie all by himself." She headed down the hall for the family living area at the back of the house. "Come on down when you finish unpacking. There's nothing Maude likes better than watching someone eat her cooking."

An hour later Alice stood in the shadows of the archway and watched Clayton as he got down on all fours and looked under all the furniture in the front parlor. He patted rugs, checked under pillows, and even peeked into lampshades. He searched flowerpots, inside Aunt Maude's tiny seashell box, and inside the piano bench. When he picked up the poker and started to shift through the ashes of last night's fire, she stepped into the room. "Looking for something?"

He turned from the fireplace and smiled. "Actually, yes." He replaced the poker in its stand. "Have you seen my glasses?"

"What glasses?"

"I seem to have misplaced them last night." Clayton glanced once again at the rug where he had awakened.

"I'm sorry, Clayton, but you weren't wearing any glasses last night."

"I know, but I should have . . . uh, arrived with them on." He didn't want to get too definite about last night, in case Alice started to ask questions he couldn't answer. She had been oddly quiet about how he had arrived, and he considered that an unusual characteristic in a woman. Most women he knew would be demanding answers, explanations, and instant replays. Alice was beginning to intrigue him as much as his missing glasses.

"You didn't *arrive* with them," she said.

"I didn't?" He glanced around the room and frowned. Where in the hell had his glasses ended up? They should have been on him, or at least nearby. Concerned, he asked, "Do you think maybe Maude or Herbert found them?"

"I'm sure they would have said something if they had." She walked into the room and straightened the pillows on the settee. "Are they that important to you?"

He jammed his hands into the back pocket of his jeans. How could he possibly explain the ramifications of them being on his nose while he'd hurled through space? He'd ended up in this parlor and they hadn't. The possibilities were endless. They could be anywhere, or nowhere at all. Wherever they are, he could have landed there himself. What if they had indeed crossed over into another dimension? Some of his colleagues believed there could be as many as twenty-six dimensions, not just the four—length, width, depth, and time—most folks were familiar with.

"The glasses themselves can be replaced," he said. "I'm just curious as to where they ended up."

"Don't you know where they are?"

Clayton felt himself flush a brilliant red. Damn if she didn't make it sound as if he didn't know what he had been doing. "I told you I have a bad habit of misplacing things."

He knew perfectly well what he had done and how he had done it. The missing glasses was a small setback, and the fact that the main computer on the teleportation machine had gone completely berserk after the test run was a major setback, but it was the fact that he hadn't landed where he was supposed to that had the team troubled. The first test run hadn't been as successful as he had initially hoped. In fact one could consider it a washout. The majority of their strategy had to be scrubbed, and they were starting over from square one. What was the use of a teleportation device if you couldn't control where you were sending anything?

He saw Alice glance down at the rug where he had landed less than twenty-four hours ago. "Clayton?"

"What?"

"Is there another reason why you're here, besides needing a place to lose stuff in?" She curiously placed a foot on the exact spot where he had lain. After a few seconds, during which she stood motionless, she took a deep breath and stepped onto the huge faded-pink cabbage rose that marked the spot. Again she stood still, frowning. Her frown deepened as she started to hop up and down.

"Alice, what are you doing?" Clayton asked, concerned. He would be the first to admit that he didn't understand the workings of the female mind, but this was just too much.

She pushed back a lock of hair and glared at him. "Just making sure."

"Sure of what?"

"That there isn't some hole into time or something in the middle of Maude's parlor." She placed her hands on her hips and demanded, "Is that why you're here, to see what made this spot so special?"

Understanding dawned, and Clayton released a small chuckle. "No, Alice. There are no holes into time." His brows pulled together for a moment in thought. "At least we don't have any proof that there are." He smiled reassuringly as a look of panic passed over her face. "I'm sure they would have been discovered long before now if there were."

"For some strange reason that doesn't fill me with confidence." As nonchalantly as possible she stepped away from the cabbage rose. "I want your word of honor as a scientist that nothing is happening in this room. I want your word that Maude and Herbert are perfectly safe."

"My being here has nothing to do with what happened last night. This house"—he spread his arms wide—"this room, is the same as it has always been." He smiled. "Your aunt and uncle are perfectly safe, you have my word as a scientist on it."

Alice nodded once. "Good, then you may stay." She closed the seashell box that he had left open. "If I find out you're lying, I will personally show you something I can do with my foot that would defy every law of physics you ever knew." She nodded again and walked toward the archway.

"I have one question for you, Alice."

She stopped and turned. "What's that?"

"Why my word of honor as a scientist instead of a man?" It annoyed him that she thought of him as a scientist first and a man second.

"I know enough about your reputation as a scientist to believe you would honor your word."

"What about the fact that I'm a man?"

A touch of sadness clouded her face. "I'll try not to hold that against you." With her shoulders straight and her chin held high, she walked out of the room.

THREE

As quietly as possible, Clayton closed and locked the door behind him. It was after midnight and he didn't want to wake anyone. A small smile teased one corner of his mouth as he turned off the porch light. No one had ever left a porch light burning for him before. It was a warm sensation, knowing someone had actually cared enough to realize he wasn't home yet and had left the light burning for him. Even if it had been a seventy-year-old woman named Maude.

Though he had been only sixteen when his parents were killed in an automobile accident, he hadn't been living at home for years. When he was four, he had been labeled as gifted. His parents had been astonished by the verdict. They wanted a nice, normal family, wanted to raise him as a normal child. Especially since, after his birth, the doctors had told his mother there wouldn't be any more children. So they kept him at home, enrolling him in the local public school. By the time he was eight, though, he was doing eighth-grade work, and his parents had to agree with his teachers that the public school couldn't offer him the education he deserved. His parents had then stood by him with love and understanding as he underwent a battery of specialized tests. When the results came back showing he had genius-level intelligence, they agreed to enroll him in a private school two hundred miles away. Within weeks his father managed to get a transfer, and his parents moved closer to his school. For the next seven years he attended classes during the week, then went home every weekend, where he was surrounded by love and family.

Now he'd been given the chance to interact once again with a family. The love that Alice, Maude, and Herbert shared was as obvious as the love his parents had had for each other and for him.

After living with the Jorgensens for a couple of days, he was beginning to know their patterns. Maude was your typical early-to-bed, early-to-rise type. She spent her days cooking, taking care of the small forest that had taken over her home, and generally fussing over everyone. Herbert spent his days napping, doing small jobs around the house, and trying to eat everything Maude cooked.

Alice was harder to pigeonhole. The first morning he had joined the family for breakfast, he nearly hadn't recognized her when she walked into the room. She had worn a pair of glasses that covered half her face and had distorted the vividness of her sky-blue eyes so that they looked lifeless and washed out. Her drab-colored business suit, high-collared blouse, and no-nonsense shoes had hid her desirable figure better than all that white fur had on Halloween. She'd pulled her gorgeous hair back into a bun so tight, he was amazed she hadn't yanked the hair out. She went to work every day dressed like that, like some Victorian schoolmarm. Alice worked in a costume that was just as conspicuous to him as the White Rabbit's outfit had been. He couldn't fathom why a woman as naturally beautiful as she would go around hiding the fact.

It was just another confusing idiosyncrasy he could add to the growing heap he had already compiled about her. Why didn't she question him about his work? Why didn't she demand more answers about his appearance Halloween night? Why didn't she want to talk about her parents? And why in the hell was she avoiding him?

Clayton shook his head and headed for the kitchen. Why was he standing in a dark hallway trying to figure out someone who obviously didn't want to be figured out, when his stomach was growling loudly enough to wake everyone in the house? Maude had promised to save him something from dinner.

He grinned when he opened the refrigerator and saw a plate piled high with roast beef, potatoes, and string beans. The plate was covered in plastic wrap, and taped to that was a note with his name and microwave directions neatly printed on it. Maude certainly knew the way to a man's heart, directly through his stomach. Her niece, however, was another story. He was definitely building up an appetite where she was concerned, but what he was hungering for wasn't any part of the four major food groups.

Clayton placed the plate in the microwave and pushed the appropriate buttons. Now he couldn't even heat up his dinner without thinking about Alice. Was it any wonder he was falling behind in his work? That afternoon he had been caught daydreaming over a simple math calculation that any second-year calculus student could have done in his sleep. Two of his fellow scientists had asked if he was feeling all right, and Dr. Madison, the only scientist on the team with a medical degree, had looked at him funny for the rest of the day. All because he had been wondering what Alice's kisses would taste like.

With a rueful shake of his head, he pulled the heated dinner from the microwave and placed it on a tray, along with two buttermilk biscuits, a small bowl of salad, and a soda he had found in the refrigerator. He carried the tray toward the family room at the back of the house. He didn't feel like eating in either the kitchen or the more formal dining room. The family room was his favorite room in the house. It had a fireplace, comfortable, worn chairs and a couch, and more books than a small-town library. The Jorgensen brothers had believed in collecting books, all kinds of books. Over the last three days he had discovered books on space travel, airplane mechanics, and animal dentistry; UFOs, aborigines, and the Holy Grail. And he had only gone through about one-twentieth of the room. If he ever got stranded on a desert island, he wanted this room to go with him.

He smiled when he saw a lamp was on and a fire was burning low in the fireplace. Someone had read his mind. He carried the tray toward the small table next to a comfortable chair, but froze when he was only halfway across the room. There on the couch, sound asleep, with a book dangling from her fingertips, was Alice.

She was wearing black leggings with thick purple socks and a baggy purple sweater. Her hair was spread out across the faded blue-plaid couch, and the golden tresses captured and reflected the glow of the flames dancing merrily in the fireplace. His gaze moved to her mouth as desire tightened his body. Her lips were parted, as if they were waiting for a lover's touch. Never in his life had he wanted to kiss a woman as much as he wanted to kiss Alice.

With a heavy sigh he forced himself to place the tray on the small table and hunt for a book to read. He grabbed the first one his fingers touched. Unable to resist, he took a step closer to Alice and glanced at the title of the book she'd been reading. A huge grin spread across his face as he sat in one of the overstuffed chairs next to the table. It was too much of a coincidence not to believe Alice hadn't heard the rumors flying around the campus about his work. She had been reading a classic, H. G. Wells's *The Time Machine*.

For the next ten minutes he sat there with a book open on his lap, eating his dinner, and studying Alice. Although he was enjoying watching her as she slept, he regretted not being able to see her eyes. Eyes he knew could sparkle and shine brighter than any diamond. Eyes he also knew she preferred to hide behind thick glasses. He glanced at the book in her hand and frowned. She obviously didn't need to wear the glasses, or she would have them on now, wouldn't she?

His gaze explored her flawless complexion, the natural hint of pink on her cheeks, the lush, deep pink of her lips, and the wave of hair that looked like sun-kissed silk. Her nose was just a trifle too narrow and her mouth was too generous to be considered classical, but she had an air of exquisite beauty surrounding her. Alice didn't need makeup to enhance her beauty. For how could you improve on natural perfection? Even in sleep she looked like an angel.

He shifted restlessly in his seat as he bit into a buttermilk biscuit. What was it about this woman that fascinated him so completely? His gaze lowered to the gentle rise and fall of her chest, and he felt the sexual pull of desire. Muttering a soft oath, he shifted his weight again. The woman had to be a witch. How else could she seduce him without even being awake? Maybe she had cast a spell over him on Halloween. That would at least explain the erotic dreams he'd had that night and every night since. He shouldn't be having *those* types of dreams. He was thirty-four years old. Old enough to control his hormones and his dreams. He scowled at the enticing length of her legs. They appeared longer now than in his dreams. *Impossible!* He felt his blood warm and rush to his groin. *She's a witch. A seductive witch who was tying his guts into huge knots and turning his life upside down!*

Alice opened her eyes at that moment, as he was glaring at her. She blinked rapidly, and the book slipped from her fingers.

Clayton jerked his gaze away from her and stared unseeingly at the open book in his lap. He waited a couple of thundering heartbeats before looking up with what he hoped was a friendly smile. "Ah, you're awake."

She pushed her hair away from her cheek and sat up. Glancing around the room, she frowned. "What time is it?"

"About twelve-thirty." He hid his grin as she bent down, picked up the book she had dropped, and tried nonchalantly to hide it from his view. "I didn't expect to find you home."

"Why not? I live here."

"It's Friday night." He watched as the glaze of sleepiness disappeared from her gaze and confusion took over.

"So?" She shook her head slightly.

"I thought you would be out with a boyfriend." Her confusion grew, and he frowned. He knew she wasn't married, and there wasn't any possessive fiancé hanging around that he had seen. Now she appeared not to even have a boyfriend. What were the men in this town, blind or just plain stupid? Anyone with half a brain and one good eye couldn't fail to notice what a fascinating contradiction she was. Prim and proper one moment, sexy as some mythical nymph the next. Alice Jorgensen just cried out to be explored. Surprised, he asked, "Surely you date?"

Her chin inched up a notch and her gaze lost its confused look. Blue flames danced dangerously in the depths of her eyes. "Of course I date, if that's any of your business. If I recall correctly, Maude said you were working late, not painting the town red."

"Painting the town red?" He hadn't heard that expression since . . . hell, he never heard anyone say that. He felt a chuckle in the back of his throat and smartly swallowed it. The look she was giving him should have singed the hair off his body. "I didn't mean to imply you couldn't get a date. I was just surprised that someone like you didn't have one, that's all."

"What's that supposed to mean?" Her fingers curled into tight fists.

Clayton smiled. She was electrifying when riled. From the slash of color highlighting her cheeks to the stubborn tilt of her chin. Desire yanked in any slack and tightened its hold. Over the years he had learned two things about the opposite sex. Never make promises he couldn't keep, and give a woman honesty. His relationships consisted of mutual physical need, respect, and the understanding that that was all it could ever be. No woman could compete with the fascination or aspiration he felt for his work. He wasn't even going to think about Alice and promises in the same breath, but he could give her the honesty. "It means I find you very attractive and extremely desirable. I'm having a hard time picturing you sitting home all by yourself on a gorgeous Friday night reading some book."

She glanced away from him and studied the orange flames in the fireplace. "This is the nineties, Dr. Williams. A woman doesn't have to have the company of a man to have an enjoyable evening."

His eyes narrowed fractionally. "I didn't imply she did." His fingers toyed with the pages of the book lying in his lap. Honesty was a hell of a thing. For the first time in three days he was getting an honest emotion from Alice besides the fear he had witnessed the night of his unannounced arrival. It was a pleasant surprise to see some emotion other than bland politeness in those captivating blue eyes. "So, Alice Jorgensen, chief information specialist at Harper University's Research Center, why have you been avoiding me?"

Her gaze jerked back to him. "I haven't been!"

He raised one eyebrow knowingly. "Haven't you?"

"How could I be avoiding you when I live here?" She kept her chin tilted defiantly, but her gaze had dropped from his to the blue-striped collar of his shirt.

"In the three days that I have lived here," he said, "you've joined us for breakfast once, and I've only caught glimpses of you heading out the front door or disappearing into your bedroom." He closed his book and his finger started to tap its cover. "Do I make you nervous, Alice?"

She clutched a beige pillow that had a Sopwith Camel needlepointed across it. "Is there a reason why I should be nervous?"

He flashed a smile and noticed that she didn't directly answer the question. "Absolutely not. I just thought since we work at the same place, we could become friends."

"I'm employed by the university to work in the library, and you're probably being paid by some government grant to do God knows what in some top-secret lab. I hardly think that constitutes being co-workers."

"You're right. Friendship should come from something we have in common."

"Such as?"

Clayton glanced around the room. "Books!" He raised the book that had been on his lap. "We both seem to love books."

She was silent for a moment. "I guess we do have that in common." She stood up, stretched, and jammed the book she had been reading into one of the many overcrowded shelves. She turned toward Clayton and tried to smother a yawn. "You won't think I'm avoiding you if I call it a night, will you?"

Clayton stood up, dropped his book into the chair, and reached for the tray piled with empty dishes. "I think I'll join you," he said, then wished he hadn't phrased it quite that way. His hormones were active enough.

Alice placed the fire screen in front of the fireplace. Most of the flames had died down and only a log or two was glowing red. There was a slight tremble to her voice as she asked, "What book were you reading?"

He couldn't very well tell her he hadn't a clue and that he had only been using it as a decoy. "It's one of the best books I've read in a long time. Simply fascinating." It seemed like a safe statement. Every book he had seen so far in the room had been fascinating.

She reached over and picked up his book. A loud laugh emerged from her throat and she shook her head. "I think we have less in common than you think, Dr. Williams."

"It's Clayton." He shifted the tray to one hand and reached for the book she still held. Embarrassment swept over him as he read the title: *The Reproductive System of the Horseshoe Crab*.

Alice continued to laugh as she bid him good night and left him standing in the center of the room clutching the book.

Alice smothered a yawn as she hurried down the stairs and headed for the kitchen. Sleep had been a long time coming the night before, and when it had finally arrived, it had carried with it the same disturbing dreams she had been experiencing since Clayton's arrival. Seductive, erotic dreams filled with hot whispers and hotter sex.

The tantalizing smell of pancakes and coffee filled the hallway and forced her mind away from the dreams. She didn't need a calendar to tell her it was Saturday morning. Maude had been making pancakes every Saturday morning since she could remember. She entered the kitchen, then stopped dead in her tracks as she took in the sight before her.

Herbert was sitting at the table wolfing down pancakes and Maude was fluttering around the stove. It was the same scene that had greeted her for fifteen years of Saturdays, with one major difference. Underneath the kitchen sink was a man. Three-quarters of perfect masculinity wrapped in denim and a maroon sweatshirt were lying across the linoleum floor. The top quarter was hidden in the cabinet beneath the sink, banging away on something and muttering. Her gaze traveled up from the tips of worn canvas sneakers, across faded denim caressing muscular thighs, to rest on the intriguing bulge nestled between those thighs. Her mouth went dry. She would have recognized that bulge anywhere. *Clayton!* She watched, entranced, as his sweatshirt worked its way upward with his every movement, leaving a thin slice of tantalizing flesh showing above the brass snap on his jeans.

"There she is!" Clayton cried triumphantly.

Alice jumped back, embarrassed that she had been caught gawking. "What are you doing under there?" she demanded.

A loud thud came from under the sink, followed by a muttered oath. Clayton slid the rest of his body out from under the sink while rubbing his forehead. "Lord, woman, must you yell so?"

"You yelled at me first," Alice snapped. She bent down and pulled his hand from his forehead. A red mark was forming there. She didn't like the feeling of guilt that assailed her because he'd bumped his head. And she surely wasn't going to like the university's reaction if she caused the boy wonder from M.I.T. to suffer a concussion. "What in tarnation were you doing under there?"

He remained perfectly still as she examined his forehead. When he sucked in a breath as her fingers stroked his brow, she realized it was the first time she had actually touched him.

"Is he all right?" asked Maude, who had left her frying pan to see for herself. Herbert took the opportunity to swipe another pancake from the plate in the middle of the table.

"I'm fine," Clayton said, still staring into Alice's eyes.

"Are you sure?" Alice asked. The slight swelling

didn't appear to be severe, but one could never tell with a head injury.

"Of course he's sure, dear," Maude answered. "He's a doctor, you know." She turned back to the skillet and deftly flipped the three cooking pancakes.

Alice held Clayton's gaze, looking for any sign of pain. Her breath caught in the back of her throat as his heated gaze bore into her. She forgot all about her aunt standing five feet behind her flipping pancakes and her uncle consuming more calories than an NFL linebacker. There was only Clayton sitting on the floor devouring her with his eyes. He seemed to be looking into her soul, searching for answers. Heat poured through her body, causing a whirlpool of fiery need to swirl in her stomach. A need that frightened more than it excited her. Her fingers trembled against his brow. Clayton was the wrong man for her to need. He was a dreamer, a man who would always search for answers and reach for the impossible. He would never be satisfied with what was in front of him, he would always want more. He was a man just like her ex-fiancé, James.

The thought of James brought Alice back to earth with a thud. She blinked rapidly as the morning sun streamed in through the window, bathing Clayton in golden light. He wore a look of baffling curiosity, like a little boy who'd just been handed a puzzle with no directions on how to figure it out. She dropped her hand as if she'd been burned. She didn't want to pique Clayton's curiosity. She needed to put a healthy distance between them.

"I think you'll live," she said. She held out a hand

and helped him to stand up. "What were you doing under there?"

He held her hand a moment longer than necessary. His thumb grazed the pulse thundering in her wrist. A knowing smiled played at the corners of his mouth before he turned away and closed the cabinet doors. He turned on the faucet and started to wash his hands. "I was seeing where the leak was coming from."

Alice blinked. "What leak?"

"The leak I told you about the other day," said Maude as she placed the cooked pancakes onto the pile already sitting on the table. She sat down and smiled at Clayton. "Breakfast is ready, young man."

Alice felt the color drain from her face. "You asked Dr. Williams to look at the plumbing?" Dear Lord, what was her aunt thinking?

"Of course I didn't ask him to look at the plumbing. He's a boarder, dear, not a handyman."

He's a genius working on space travel without the damn spaceship! Alice groaned. How was she ever going to explain that to Maude when her aunt still thought he was a medical doctor. Suddenly breakfast lost most of its appeal.

"Maude's right, Alice," Clayton said. "She didn't ask me to look. I volunteered to see what I could find while she finished cooking breakfast."

"If the leak's that bad, I'll call a plumber right after breakfast," Alice said.

Clayton shook his head. "No need for that. I've already figured out what the problem is and can have it fixed before lunch."

Alice's fork stopped in mid-air as she was reaching for a pancake. "You can't possibly fix the leak."

Clayton frowned. "Why not?"

She could think of a million reasons why a man with a doctorate degree from M.I.T. should not be fooling around with their plumbing. "Don't you have to get to work?" seemed the safest response.

"Not today." He grinned. "The team voted to take a weekend off. We've been working seven days a week, over fourteen hours a day, for the past two months. We needed a break." He handed Maude his cup and winked. "It's my understanding that the other scientists' spouses were conspiring together on some plan if we didn't break for the weekend."

"I should say," said Maude as she poured coffee for everyone.

"That's all the more reason why you shouldn't be fixing some stupid drain on your first day off," Alice said. She glanced at Clayton. Did he have to look so damn appealing without even trying? He didn't strike her as a man who was obsessed with appearances. His hair was on the longish side and his clothes, while clean and neat, weren't the latest fashion. She had seen him more with stubble on his jaw than without. He reminded her of someone with a lot more on his mind than impressing people. So why was he offering to fix Maude's leak?

"She has a point there," Herbert mumbled around a mouthful of pancakes. "I'll have another look after breakfast."

"You already looked three times," said Maude. "And

not once could you see the leak, never mind where the leak was coming from."

"I'll call the plumber," Alice said. The last time Herbert played with the plumbing, he had flooded out one of the upstairs bathrooms and it had cost her a small fortune in water damage. Maude refused to take board money from her, so over the years she had been financing the major repairs needed on the house. Last year she paid for a brand-new roof and gutters. This year she was hoping to have enough saved to replace the ancient furnace and put in an efficient heating system.

"I think since it's my day off, I should be able to do with it as I want," Clayton said.

"Why, of course," Maude said as she passed him the pitcher of orange juice. "A man who works as hard as you do deserves it."

"Good." Clayton nodded once and dug into the mound of food in front of him.

"What are you going to do?" asked Maude.

Clayton flashed her a wide grin. "I'm going to fix your leak."

Maude chuckled and delicately forked into her breakfast. "I hope you like chocolate cake, young man. Because I'm going to bake one today that doesn't come from a box."

Alice muttered a dark comment as she stabbed at her meal. She couldn't fight all of them. Let him work under some smelly sink all day replacing washers, gaskets, or whatever it was that caused drains to leak.

Maude glanced at Clayton, then at her niece. "What are you going to do today, Alice?"

"I have to go into town this morning to drop off some dry cleaning and pick up a few things." She finished her coffee and stood up. Most of her meal lay uneaten on her plate. "I have to get going if I want to be back before lunch. Do you need anything?"

"Not today, dear," Maude said. Herbert only shook his head.

"Then I'm off," she said as she walked out of the room. She didn't once look at Clayton.

Three minutes later she was closing her bedroom door and heading down the upstairs hall when her feet slowed. Clayton was standing at the top of the stairs waiting for her. She shifted the pile of clothes she had gathered for the dry cleaners. Short of pushing him out of the way, there was nothing she could do but stop and talk to the man. She halted a safe couple of feet away. "Can I help you with something, Clayton?" She noticed that his hair covered most of the red mark on his forehead.

He jammed his hands into his pockets. "You're avoiding me again."

"I am not." She took a step closer just to prove to herself she could. A sweet ache tormented her stomach at the look of distress clouding his face. He looked like he wasn't sure what to say next. She softened her tone. "I go into town every Saturday morning."

"Then you won't mind if I tag along." He stepped away from the railing and moved nearer to her.

She felt the urge to move away, but held her ground. "I thought you were fixing the leak."

He closed the final step between them and slowly

raised a finger to her lower lip. "I need to pick up some parts."

Alice had no idea what they were talking about, but she knew it wasn't the plumbing. The heat of his finger seemed to scorch her mouth. She raised her eyes and encountered his hungry gaze. She saw his intent before he started to lower his head. He was going to kiss her! "I don't think . . ."

He removed his finger from her lips and his mouth brushed hers. "Don't think, Alice." His lips teased the corner of her mouth. "Just feel."

FOUR

Alice stopped at the red light and cautiously snuck a peek at the man sitting beside her. She didn't know what upset her the most; that he had the gall to kiss her, or that the kiss had been so fleeting, she might have imagined it if it hadn't been for the heat that incinerated the walls of her stomach. One moment he was brushing the sweetest kiss she had ever tasted across her mouth and telling her to feel, and the next he was asking her to wait for him while he got his jacket from his bedroom.

She pulled away as the light turned green, and started to look for a parking space. Saturday mornings on Main Street were crowded. Over the years the university had grown in size and esteem, but Main Street had remained Main Street. Grundy's Hardware Store still catered to most of the same clientele that had walked through its doors the day it opened back in 1955; Sam's Sandwich Shop still made the best turkey melt; and Clyde's Barber Shop still preferred to do crew cuts rather than the latest craze of shaving designs onto one's head. Harper's National Bank had been bought out by some statewide conglomerate two years earlier, but the tellers were the same friendly people who had been cashing Alice's checks since her first job of dishing out ice cream at the local Dairy Freeze the summer she turned sixteen.

About five years ago a mall had been built closer to the university. It contained a couple of large department stores and a multitude of specialty shops that catered to the younger college crowd. Among them was a pizza parlor, a record and book store, a drugstore, and half a dozen shops that blared loud music and brimmed with strange clothes and stranger salespeople. Alice preferred to do her business on safe, unchanging Main Street.

She turned the car into an empty spot that had just opened up in front of Anne Marie's Bakery. "The hardware store is about four stores down," she said to Clayton, gesturing toward the right. "That way." She didn't want him trailing behind her all morning and she surely didn't want to accompany him, like some love-struck adolescent, in his search for plumbing supplies. She had no idea how this ridiculous fascination with Clayton had started, but she was putting an end to it right now.

He glanced at the various stores through the windshield before turning toward her. "You aren't coming with me?"

"I don't need anything from the hardware store." She pocketed the keys and opened the car door. Was that *hurt* she had picked up in his voice? "I'm sure you can manage all by yourself." The man couldn't possibly be upset that she didn't want to go traipsing up and down aisles containing such fascinating items as Septic Tank Clean Out and Roach Motels, could he? She reached into the backseat, picked up her dry cleaning, and closed the door. She glanced at Clayton over the top of the car. Why in the heck was he looking like a little boy who was just told there was no Easter Bunny? "I'll meet you back here in about an hour." Without waiting for an answer, she hurried away before she changed her mind and spent half the morning surrounded by pyramids of paint cans, barrels full of leaf rakes, bags of rock salt, and power tools.

Clayton looked in awe at the wall filled with PVC tubing. There were pieces bent at forty-five-degree angles and ninety-degree angles. Tubes were bent into S-shapes, U-shapes, and even T-shapes. There were bins filled with valves, traps, elbows, and end caps. Three different kinds of cleaner and five different brands of adhesives filled an entire shelf. Six-, ten-, and twelve-foot lengths of tubing were jammed into an old wooden barrel and reached for the ceiling. As if the various shapes weren't mind-boggling enough, everything came in different sizes. There was half-inch, five-eighths, and even some one-inch widths of tubing.

Clayton swallowed hard, closed his eyes, said a silent prayer to the Home Repair God, then did the only thing he could. He reached for the handy little pamphlets some of the manufacturers had written up for beginners like himself. Suddenly it seemed ridiculous that he had reached the age of thirty-four without so much as having changed a washer.

Half an hour later a smiling Clayton left Grundy's Hardware Store with a bag filled with parts, tools, and half a dozen pamphlets. He stopped at Alice's car and placed his manly treasures in the backseat next to the plastic-wrapped suits Alice had already picked up from the cleaners. He shut the door and leaned against the front fender. Whoever heard of leaving one's laundry draped over the backseat of an unlocked vehicle? Alice was just begging someone to swipe her clothes. He glanced in through the window at the clear plastic bags and slowly shook his head. If someone did swipe those militant suits, which ranged in colors from muddy-creek brown to death-shroud black, it would be the best thing that could happen to her. A man would be taking his life into his hands to try to snuggle up to a woman wearing one of those suits. They radiated about as much warmth as a ten-foot icicle.

He preferred her as she was today. All warm and cuddly in an oversized sweater, faded jeans, and tasting of maple syrup and coffee. He could still feel the heat of her response to the simple kiss they had shared in the upstairs hall. It had taken everything he possessed not to deepen the kiss and show her exactly what she did to him, prudish suits and all.

Clayton glanced up and down the busy sidewalk. No sign of Alice. He surveyed the stores in front of him, trying to decide which one she might be in. With a wide grin he pushed away from the car and headed for a small shop. He had no idea if Alice would be in there, but he wanted to be. It was the shop directly in front of him, the one producing the tantalizing aroma of freshly baked cinnamon buns, Anne Marie's Bakery.

Twenty minutes later Clayton stopped in front of the Thanksgiving display taking up most of the center aisle in Harper's Drugstore and watched Alice. She was standing in front of a white metal book rack filled with paperbacks. Her teeth were worrying her lower lip as she slowly read every title. He could think of at least three different parts of his body he wouldn't mind her sinking those pearly whites into. In fact there wasn't a part on his body he wouldn't mind her giving the same treatment she was lavishing on her lower lip. He shifted his hold on the three bakery boxes he was carrying and wondered how she managed to look so tempting while browsing through the latest best-sellers. He took a deep breath before walking over and standing directly behind her. "Looking for anything in particular?"

She jumped and spun around. "Clayton!"

He raised an eyebrow. "Who else were you expecting?" He studied the glossy covers on the books before them. Some displayed more skin than a nudist colony, others were a virtual field of flowers, one had an empty cradle, and still another showed some poor man lying facedown with a blood-soaked ax embedded in his back. Interesting selection.

"I thought you were in the hardware store," she said.

"I was." He picked up a book with an enticing portrait of a scantily dressed woman with enormous breasts overflowing her low-cut gown, gleaming thighs surrounded by an eyelet petticoat yanked almost up to her waist, and some rakehell of a pirate holding her in all the right places. He handed it to Alice with a grin. "This one looks good."

A tide of red swept up Alice's cheeks as she jammed the book back onto the rack. "That's not the kind of book I had in mind."

He glanced at the book wistfully. The blonde on the cover sort of resembled Alice. "What kind did you have in mind?"

Alice moved away from the book rack. "Obviously one they don't carry here." She shifted the red plastic basket she was carrying farther away from him. "Did you find what you were looking for?"

"Yes, Maude's sink will be fixed before lunch." He stood beside her as she surveyed the Thanksgiving decorations and eyed the contents of her basket. A selection of woman's necessities greeted his gaze. Three packages of pantyhose, moisturizer, two bottles of shampoo and conditioner, a box of tampons, and a deodorant that was made for a woman took up half the basket. He looked at the last items lying in the basket and grinned. Either Alice was buying Christmas presents early, or he had just spotted a weakness in her character. Three boxes of coconut cream patties attested to a very sweet tooth.

"Are you going to be here for a few more minutes?" he asked.

"Sure. Go ahead and do whatever it is you want to do." She waved her hand toward the door and maneuvered the basket even farther to her side. "I'll meet you at the car in a little while." She picked up a pair of orange candles with decals of little pilgrims wrapped around their base.

"Oh, I don't have to go anywhere. I just thought since I'm here I could pick up some stuff I'm running low on." He walked the few steps to the front of the store and picked up a red basket of his own. "You don't mind, do you?"

"It's a free country." She placed the candles into her basket and hurriedly tossed in a package of paper napkins with colorful turkeys printed on them. The napkins landed directly on the box of tampons she was trying to hide.

Clayton glanced at her basket and smiled knowingly before moving to the next aisle, where the men's grooming products were sandwiched in between every conceivable color nail polish manufactured on earth and pink bottles of Mr. Bubble. All these years he had listened to his colleagues and avoided shopping with a woman, only to discover how intriguing it could be. Alice's choices told him a lot about herself. The absence of makeup and perfumes confirmed his opinion that she was a natural beauty, and her choice of shampoo was an inexpensive brand. Not that she probably couldn't afford all the glitz and glimmer of womanhood, but he had a feeling it just wasn't important to her.

Now, the coconut cream patties could be another story. All three silver-foiled boxes contained expensive and sinfully rich hand-dipped patties. He'd wager all the money in his wallet that the candies cost more than everything else she had in her basket.

He tossed a can of shaving cream and a package of

razor blades into his basket, then got in line behind Alice as she started to check out. The cashier seemed to know her very well.

"I see you found the chocolates Ralph ordered in especially for you," the cheerful woman said as she punched the amount of each box into the old relic of a cash register.

"Yes, I wanted to thank him but he's not behind the counter." Alice glanced over at the empty pharmaceutical counter.

"He's over at Jimmy's getting a haircut." The cashier continued to thump on the numbers of the temperamental register. "One of these days I'm going to retire this thing and have one of those fancy scanner things installed."

Alice laughed and replaced the now-empty basket on the stack next to her. "That will be the day, Sylvia." She handed a couple of bills to the cashier. "Ralph and you both love this place just the way it is."

Sylvia handed back some change and slammed the cash drawer twice before it closed properly. "How do you know?"

Alice dropped the change into her purse and reached for her bags. "Because if you didn't, you would have changed it long ago."

Sylvia grumbled something and glanced at Clayton. "Did you find everything you needed, young man?"

Clayton gave a low grunt of pleasure as Alice accidentally backed into him. Heat shot through his body as her firm little tush brushed against a part of his anatomy he had been trying to repress since meeting her. He managed a small smile. "Everything I need is right here." He handed the cashier his basket, but continued to look at Alice.

Sylvia glanced between him and Alice, no doubt noticing the red sweeping up Alice's face. She chuckled as she jabbed the amount of his razor blades into the register. "You two know each other?"

"Definitely," Clayton said.

Alice stepped away from the counter and from Clayton. "Sylvia, I would like you to meet Dr. Williams. He's working at the university and boarding at our house for the next couple of weeks."

Clayton raised an eyebrow and shot Alice an amused look. "It could be months, perhaps even years."

Sylvia continued to chuckle and thump away at the register.

"Years?" Alice whispered.

He casually shrugged. "What I do isn't an exact science. The going consensus is it will take a couple of lifetimes even to begin to understand the process."

"What exactly do you do, Dr. Williams?" Sylvia asked.

"I'm doing research on Einstein's theory of relativity."

"Oh, you're a mathematician."

"Something like that," Clayton muttered. Saying he was a mathematician was like saying Michelangelo dabbled with paints. Neither one was a complete lie, but it didn't portray a whole picture. A lot of his job depended highly on mathematics, along with a heavy dose of quantum physics, knowledge of physical laws of time and space, and a hell of a lot of luck. Space travel wasn't an exact science; it required a broad base of knowledge in many different areas. Telling people who questioned his work that he was working on Einstein's theory of relativity was a safe, pat answer. Not only was Einstein so highly respected that no one thought twice about someone following in his footsteps, but not many people had enough knowledge of his theory of relativity to question Clayton further about his work.

He glanced at the total showing on the register and handed Sylvia a twenty. As she was giving him back his change, he spotted a small rack of candy. On impulse he picked up two coconut cream–filled candy bars. "I'll take these also, please."

Sylvia rang up the two candy bars and dropped them into his bag. Her glance slid to Alice, who was standing by the door staring outside. She handed Clayton his change and whispered, "Smart move."

Clayton's glance slid between Sylvia and Alice. "I was playing a hunch."

Sylvia handed him the bag. "If you ever get bored with mathematics, you should try a career in policework."

"I'll keep that in mind."

Clayton was still chuckling as he joined Alice and opened the door. Cool, brisk air hit them face on as they stepped onto the sidewalk. The smell of burning leaves and woodstoves penetrated the fall air. Autumn was a wonderful time of the year, Clayton mused. With any luck he'd get Alice in front of the fireplace tonight and discuss something else they have in common besides their love of books. He was hoping to discuss the fleeting kiss they had shared. More accurately he was hoping to do a heck of a lot more than discuss it. He was planning to dissect it into microscopic particles. First there was the heat, then the texture of her mouth, then the taste of her. If she needed a refresher course, he'd be more than happy to demonstrate.

As they headed for the car, though, he intercepted a hard glare from Alice. "You shouldn't make fun of Sylvia," she said, "just because she was polite enough to believe your lie about being a mathematician."

The smile of anticipation slid from Clayton's face. "You think I'm having a good laugh at Sylvia's expense?" he asked, hurt.

"Aren't you?"

"No." He stopped in the middle of the sidewalk and stared at her. How in the hell could she have thought such a thing? Had he really been considering sharing a candy bar with her just so he could witness how much passion she had for chocolate and coconut cream? "We were sharing a private joke."

"About what?"

He toyed with the brown bag clutched in his hand, glanced at the seductive pout of her lower lip, and grinned. "If I told you, it wouldn't be private, would it?" He started to whistle a snappy little tune as he continued on to the car.

Alice paced the dining room, cringing every time she heard Clayton mutter something in German. She had no idea what he was saying, but she had a feeling Maude wouldn't appreciate having such language used in her house, let alone in her kitchen. The simple plumbing job that was only going to take minutes had been going on for three hours. She had peeked into the room twenty minutes ago. Herbert and their neighbor, George Ingels, had taken up residence at either side of the kitchen sink and were sprouting advice and opinions faster than a politician during election year. Alice presumed most of Clayton's comments were directed to his two helpers and not to the ancient pipes beneath the sink.

She really should go in there and help him by shooing away Herbert and George, but then she would have to face Clayton. And confronting Clayton was something she wasn't looking forward to doing. The twelve-block drive home from Main Street had been a nightmare. Clayton had whistled and hinted at some private joke between him and Sylvia all the way. A joke that concerned her.

What in the world could Sylvia possibly say that concerned her? Clayton was the one who should be shot for telling sweet, nice Sylvia he was a mathematician. What a crock. She could understand his reasoning for secrecy, but did he have to act so giddy about it? And since when did grown men act giddy?

Alice frowned at the archway leading into the kitchen as more German words blistered the air. She had a sinking feeling she knew what those words meant. Taking a deep breath, she walked into the tool-cluttered kitchen. She wasn't positive, but she could swear she smelled testosterone hanging in the air.

She glanced at Herbert and George sitting inches away from the sink, and her sympathy for Clayton reached an all-time high. Three-quarters of his gorgeous body was crammed and twisted under the sink like some deformed pretzel. If she hadn't recognized his worn sneaker attached to the one leg not jammed into the cabinet, she would never have known it was he.

"You should try the monkey wrench," Herbert said. He picked up the heavy tool and practically shoved it into the cabinet.

"No, no," George said as he grabbed the tool out of Herbert's hand. "What he needs to do is replace the entire trap section." He tapped Clayton on the knee. "Do you see where the thingamajig connects with the doodad?"

"Don't listen to him, Clayton," said Herbert as he leaned in closer. "The last time he crawled under his sink was when a loaf of bread cost thirty-nine cents."

"Look who's talking!" George snapped. "The last time he tried to fix a leak, he flooded the entire bathroom so bad that it leaked through the floorboards and damaged the plaster ceiling in the dining room."

Clayton muttered another curse as his hand slipped off the wrench and whacked into the pipe. "Would you two cut it out. I'm perfectly capable of fixing a simple leak by myself." He repositioned the wrench and tried to keep his shoulder from blocking what little light filtered into the shadowy cabinet. Between clenched teeth he muttered, "Why don't you two go turn on the television in the other room and watch the football game? I heard Notre Dame's playing Penn State."

"But who would hand you the tools?" Herbert asked.

"I will," Alice answered. She had seen and heard enough to realize that without too much more provocation, Clayton would probably take the monkey wrench to her uncle and their neighbor and fix their plumbing. Particularly their leaky mouths.

"What do you know about being a plumber's helper?" asked Herbert.

"I know enough to leave the poor man alone while he's working." She glanced at the tools scattered across the beige-and-gold linoleum floor and the countertops. There was even a hammer sitting on the kitchen table. It looked like Herbert and George had had a tool fight and the tools had won.

"Alice, could you please hand me the flashlight?" Clayton asked.

With a triumphant smile she picked up the red plastic flashlight, turned it on, and placed it in Clayton's outstretched hand. "See, I can manage. Why don't you two run along and watch the game?" She glanced at the clock. "It started about twenty minutes ago." She noticed the hesitant but interested looks Herbert and George shared. "I heard they were giving Penn State a ten-point victory over Notre Dame."

"Never," sputtered George as he stood up and pushed his chair back under the table. "Penn State doesn't stand a chance."

"You tell her, George," Herbert said. "Let's go in the other room and watch it. Alice can hand Clayton the tools just as well as we can."

"I have a better idea," said George. "Let's go over to my house and watch it on my television."

"You just want to go over there because Maude's borrowing your kitchen while Clayton's working on her sink." Herbert returned his own chair and reached for his coat hanging by the back door.

"I do not," George said as he slipped on his coat and opened the door. "I just don't feel like sitting here for hours squinting at your little twenty-inch screen when I have a perfectly good twenty-seven-inch console sitting next door."

Alice chuckled as Herbert's reply was lost when the back door closed behind them. She started to pick up the scattered tools and place them all by the open toolbox sitting in the middle of the floor. It would be easier searching for any tools Clayton might need if they were all in one spot.

"Are they gone?" he asked hopefully.

"For at least a couple of hours," she said. She let her gaze travel up his one leg until it disappeared under the sink. "Can I ask you a question?"

"Sure." He grunted as he tried for the third time to loosen a section of the trap.

"How did all of you fit under there?" She took a step closer and bent over to get a better view. Clayton's face was six inches away from the chrome piping, his arms were pressed against his sides, and the flashlight was jammed between his legs with the beam shining upward at the pipe.

"Luck," he muttered as the stubborn pipe finally gave way.

"I know you're interested in the laws of physics concerning time and space, but somehow I had a feeling it was a different kind of space you were interested in." She couldn't resist the remark. He looked utterly ridiculous crammed under there. If his colleagues could see him now, they would swear he was either performing an experiment or had lost his mind.

"How would you know what I'm interested in, Alice?"

"I only—" The rest of her comment was lost as his shout of outrage filled the kitchen. Alice hurriedly dropped to her knees in front of the cabinet. She expected to see blood or some other physical sign that Clayton had hurt himself. Instead she took in the sight before her and burst out laughing. He had obviously succeeded in taking the entire trap out, only he had forgotten about the water still sitting in its curve. The water mark soaking the front of his jeans showed exactly where all that water had fallen.

She tried to muffle her laughter as Clayton started to untwist his way from beneath the cabinet. One arm emerged and gripped the edge of the counter. His bent leg slowly joined the other one. The wet spot covered him from his abdomen to the top of his thighs. The soaked flashlight slid from between his legs and dropped to the floor with a soft thud. Next came his chest and other arm. His head was the last thing to appear. She noticed the look of indignity and burst out laughing all over again. She didn't know what had upset him the most, the water soaking his pants, the fact that he had forgotten about the water, or that she had witnessed the entire accident.

"I take it you think this is amusing?"

"Amusing? No." Her grin grew larger as she scooted farther away from him on her rear. "I think *this* is hilarious."

He cocked one eyebrow, tossed the now-empty pipe back under the sink, and slid right after her. "Would you care to share the joke with me?"

Her amused glance shot to the wet patch on his pants. The water had made the heavy denim cling to his body. A very impressive body! She jerked her gaze back up, swallowed hard, and moved a couple more inches across the floor. "Well, you are a genius, you know."

"Who says?" He continued to advance on her.

She didn't like the determined gleam in his eyes. "You have an I.Q. of over one hundred and fifty." She felt the wall press against her back.

Both of his eyebrows rose in surprise. "It seems that someone has been doing her homework."

"I like to know who's living in our house. Waking up some morning and finding out our boarder is an ax murderer wouldn't make my day."

He slid the last couple of feet toward her. The denim covering their knees couldn't have been any closer unless someone sewed a seam. "If you did your research properly, you would know that I.Q. score was taken when I was eight years old." He leaned in closer. "I would hardly classify it as accurate now."

"I know when the test was given." Her glance shot between the table and chairs on her right and the refrigerator on her left. She was trapped. "I also know that you refused to be retested."

"With good reason." Pain clouded his eyes. "That stupid test changed my life."

"I know." She clutched her fingers together to prevent herself from touching him. "You were yanked out of your public school and shipped away from your family, off to a special school for gifted children."

"My parents moved closer to the school as soon as my father's transfer went through."

"By the time you were fifteen, you were attending M.I.T. By the time you were—"

He reached out and pressed a finger to her lips. "Do you work for the CIA or what?"

His finger brushed against her mouth as she whispered, "I'm an information specialist."

"A very good one at that." His finger outlined the arch of her upper lip. "Do I want to know how you dug up all that information on me?"

She shook her head. "Trade secret."

His finger slid to her lower lip and tenderly pulled down. He traced the moist inner lip. "Did your source give you any information on any of the projects I worked on?"

"Only the public ones."

"What about the one I'm working on now?"

"Listed as classified."

He raised an eyebrow at that and leaned in closer. "Really?" He replaced his finger with a fleeting sweep of his tongue. "What else did you find out?"

Desire danced in the wake of his caress. She could

feel the warmth of his breath as it feathered her face. She wanted more. Needed more. Her hungry gaze fastened on his mouth. Who cared that he was a registered Democrat, a major contributor to Greenpeace, and that he wore a size-ten shoe? "Nothing earth-shattering."

His face dipped closer until his lips brushed hers. "What do you consider earth-shattering, sweet Alice?"

Her hands unclenched and reached for his shoulders. She had waited long enough to see if his kisses were as hot and sweet as they had promised to be. The morning's encounter in the upstairs hallway seemed a lifetime ago. She pulled him closer and whispered, "Kiss me and I'll show you."

"Great galaxies," he murmured just as her mouth closed in on his.

FIVE

There were kisses, and then there were *kisses*. Alice's kisses were one of the latter, Clayton decided instantly. Her mouth was as sweet as heaven, hot as Hades, and dealt out more promises of paradise than the Bureau of Tourism for the Caribbean. He never wanted to release it. He'd known she would taste like the entrance to Eden. Known it, and feared it. Like Adam he was afraid he was going to be led down the path of temptation, only to discover he would have to pay for his sins and leave the garden. Alice needed a man who could offer her a one-hundred-percent commitment of himself. Clayton couldn't. His work had always consumed the best part of him. The pieces left were fine for brief relationships, but not for her. Alice deserved so much more than he could give.

He tried to pull away, but he only succeeded in having her tighten her hold and moan softly into his mouth. The sweet sound of her desire went straight to his head and ignited a fire hot enough to burn away every one of his good intentions. With a fiery thrust of his tongue he plunged deeper into paradise. The lush honey-sweetness of Alice consumed his senses until there was nothing left but her and this burning desire.

Alice answered the bold question Clayton's tongue was asking with shy ripostes. Her fingers wove their way into the silky depths of his hair and forced the kiss to go deeper.

With a heavy groan Clayton gave up the last of his resistance and hauled her across the floor and into his embrace. He opened his legs wide as she curled her body up against him. He could feel the heavy weight of her breasts against his chest, and one slim hip was nudging a very wet and sensitive area of his body. The heat radiating from that sensitive area was surely sending up a head of steam that could power a locomotive. Clayton released her mouth and laid a string of kisses over her jaw to her ear. His teeth lightly nipped at the delicate pink lobe. "Don't look now, but I think the earth just shifted."

She smiled as she tilted her head back, giving him better access to her throat. "I must be doing something wrong if all you're feeling is a slight shift." Her one hand left his shoulder and pressed against his heaving chest.

He felt the heat of her hand through the heavy cotton of his sweatshirt. Lord, what was he going to do? He couldn't continue this assault on his senses without following through to its natural conclusion. Yet he couldn't bring himself to stop. The heated smoothness of Alice's throat slid under his seeking mouth like hot satin. He gulped in a deep breath as the neckline of her sweater halted his progress, and the sharp tug of Alice's fingers digging into his sweatshirt caused a fresh onslaught of desire to flow into his groin. He forced his mouth away from the thundering pulse beating under her silky skin. "You're doing everything perfectly." He flexed his hips against her. "That's why it's shifting."

She nudged his straining arousal. A huge grin lit up her face. " 'Shifting'? I thought we were trying for 'earth-shattering.' "

He wrapped his arms tightly around her and held her immobile. He had reached his peak of resistance. If she pressed against him one more time, he wouldn't be able to control his potent need to make love to her. "We bypassed 'shattering' with the first kiss." His hips instinctively jerked against the temptation of her thigh. "Right about now we're working on 'explosive.' "

A quiet laugh escaped her as she buried her face in his sweatshirt. Stifling another laugh, she managed to croak out, " 'Explosive'?"

He hugged her tighter and rested his chin on top of her head. "Oh, yeah." He rolled his eyes and prayed for strength. The sweet, natural fragrance of her shampoo teased his senses as he tried to control the raging fires tearing through his body. He felt like a lone firefighter confronting an out-of-control conflagration. He couldn't begin to fathom where to start to dig the trenches.

Alice was surrounding him on all sides, leaving him precious little space to escape. She was working her magic, casting her spell, by using the most unorthodox method he had ever seen. She didn't flirt or pretend to have a great interest in his work. She never wore sexy clothes, makeup, or exotic perfumes. She hid behind thick-framed glasses and ugly suits all day, and at night she avoided him like the plague. So why was she snuggled in his arms, on a damp kitchen floor, with her cheek pressed against his rapidly pounding heart? And why would he sell his soul to the devil to make love to her this very minute?

She tried to back out of his arms, and he tightened them more securely around her. "Clayton?"

"Hmmm . . ." He knew he should have released her, but he wanted to feel her warmth a moment longer.

She pushed enough space between them to look up at him. Lifting one hand, she lightly touched his jaw with its faint stubble. "This wasn't supposed to happen."

"I know." He tried to smooth away the frown pulling on her kissable mouth. "I should stay away from you." His hungry gaze followed the path his finger had just taken. Staying away from her was the last thing he wanted to do.

She shook her head. "No, it's me who should stay away from you."

It was Clayton's turn to frown. He knew it was totally unreasonable, but her comment hurt. The best thing he could do was back off now and leave her alone. She had tasted like heaven and forever. He couldn't afford to think about forever with Alice. Some things weren't meant to be. "Why? What have I ever done to you?"

"You haven't done anything to me." She pulled her sweater down and backed out of his arms until a good twelve inches of linoleum lay between them. "It's just that you're not my type."

He raised an eyebrow and shifted his bottom on the hard floor. "How do you know what type I am?" Why was he arguing with her? Wasn't he supposed to be counting his lucky stars that she didn't find him attractive?

She pushed back a wisp of hair that had escaped her braid during their kisses. "I've seen your type before." Her teeth sank into her lower lip and her gaze fell to the middle of his chest.

"And what type am I?" He couldn't contain the hurt or the anger in his voice. Alice was grouping him with other men from her past. He was just a simple man, with simple needs. He might be a genius, one of the scientific community's wonder boys, but he was a man first. A man who didn't like to be measured by some other man's yardstick.

Apparently Alice had picked up on the hurt and anger in his voice, and she jerked her gaze back to his. "You're a dreamer," she said softly.

"A dreamer?"

"You work with things that I don't understand, that ninety-nine percent of the population wouldn't understand. Your job requires you to wade through theories thicker than pea soup and with more twists and turns than a labyrinth. You do math computations that look like some foreign language. But your mind, Clayton, is always dreaming, always reaching." She tried to smile.

"You can't be who you are without being that dreamer. You always have to be dreaming about the future and asking yourself, 'What if?' Once one mystery is solved and another door is open, you have to rush in and demand to know the secrets behind the next door. You'd never be satisfied with what you have. There's always another door to be unlocked."

Clayton shook his head and stared down into her soft blue eyes. A man could see heaven in those eyes if he tried hard enough. And against all rhyme and reason he wanted to try. "What's that got to do with you and me?" He didn't understand what she was saying. Of course he thought about the future and he did constantly ask himself, "What if?" That was part of who he was. It came to him as naturally as breathing. Being a man of science, he was always in search of one answer or another. Right now he wanted to know why Alice was physically and mentally backing away from him.

"There is no 'you and me,' Clayton." She blinked her eyes and took a deep breath. "You're a dreamer and I'm a realist."

"I'm a man and you're a woman," he growled in frustration.

She sadly shook her head and stood up.

Clayton continued to sit on the floor. "I'm not a man?"

"Of course you are." She smoothed down her sweater and toyed with the end of her braid that was draped over her shoulder.

"You're not a woman?" His gaze knowingly swept up her body. Now that he had held her in his arms and felt every sweet curve pressed against him, he knew what lay hidden beneath those baggy sweaters and ugly suits she wore. Alice might succeed in hiding herself from the rest of the world, but he knew. He knew and he wanted her.

"You're deliberately misunderstanding me." She took a bucket and a sponge from where Maude kept the cleaning supplies and started to soak up the water still lying in the bottom of the cabinet.

Clayton eyed her rounded bottom and groaned as heat tightened in his groin.

Alice poked her head out from beneath the sink. "Did you say something?"

He swallowed hard and forced a friendly smile. The woman was driving him totally insane. He had been ready to apologize for the kiss and to swear on a stack of Bibles that it would never happen again, until she'd so politely dismissed the whole incident by declaring he was a dreamer and therefore she wasn't interested. He knew she was attracted to him. He had felt it in her response. Felt it in the way her body answered every one of his unspoken questions with a resounding yes. So what did his being a dreamer, if he was such a thing, have to do with anything?

"I said not to worry too much about cleaning up under there." He stood and pulled on the damp denim clinging to his thighs. "The hard part is done. All I have to do is put the new pipes in and it will be as good as new."

She glanced over her shoulder at him. "It should be as good as new"—a teasing smile curved her mouth—

"considering it is new." She gave the bottom of the cabinet one last swipe with the sponge.

Clayton picked up the new trap and shook it at her. "Would you rather I have Herbert and George finish fixing this?" He knew when to back off a subject. Alice was acting as jittery as an actress on opening night. He'd let her have her reprieve for the time being. He was a man of science, and weren't they known for having patience?

She moved the bucket and sponge aside. "I'll call a plumber first before I'd allow Herbert to replace so much as a washer in this house."

"Then be a good sport and hand me that wrench over by the toolbox." He knelt down in front of the cabinet and, muttering "Patience," crawled inside.

Alice took a last swipe of the mop across the linoleum floor before stepping out into the hall. The kitchen sink was working perfectly, the tools and clutter had been cleaned up, and the floor shone from its recent washing. Maude would be so proud of the kitchen, but not of Alice. She was doing it again. She was hiding from life.

Six years ago she had been reaching for life, for the future, with every fiber of her being. She had graduated from Harper University with honors, was starting a promising career, and was engaged to the man who had stolen her heart during the last semester of her junior year. For the first time in her life since her parents' death, Alice had allowed herself to dream.

She glanced down at the bucket filled with dirty water, refusing to cry. Tears didn't solve a blasted thing, nor could they change the past. She hadn't been the one to kill the dream. She wasn't the one who'd walked away from the future. James was the one who'd broken off the wedding, smashed her heart, and shattered the dreams. But she should have known. James was a dreamer, and a dreamer always followed his dreams no matter who got hurt in the process. Her parents had followed their dreams, right smack into the middle of the Amazon and to their deaths, leaving behind a frightened and bewildered girl. Uncle Elmer had followed his dreams and left behind a warm and caring Maude. Uncle Alfred's dream had ended on some distant mountaintop in the Himalayas, while on expedition searching for the Abominable Snowman, before she'd even been born.

Maude had been wrong years ago when she accused Alice of hiding from life. She didn't hide from life, she had only stopped dreaming. Herbert had the right idea. If you didn't dream, you didn't get hurt. Six years ago Alice had made a vow to herself never to dream again, and never, never to get involved with another dreamer. For years she had lived by those rules. She worked, paid her taxes, shopped, made a few good friends, was a caring niece, and never once dreamed. So why all of a sudden did she feel like crying over those wasted years?

"You didn't have to wash the floor. I would have done it," Clayton said. He had come up silently behind her in the hall. His hair was still damp from his shower, and he was wearing a pair of brown twill pants and a thick cable-knit sweater.

Alice's chin jerked away from the mop handle it had been resting on. "Do you always sneak up on people so, so . . ."

"So, what?" He raised his brows in amusement.

"So suddenly!" She didn't like the idea that Clayton was always popping up on her unannounced and catching her off guard. He had done that since Halloween night, and it was about time he stopped. "If you're going to live here, have some decency and knock before entering a room."

He glanced up and down the hallway before turning his gaze back to her. "Alice, you're standing in the middle of the hallway, looking like a daydreaming Cinderella"—he glanced meaningfully at her hair and clothes—"before the ball. A herd of elephants could have snuck up on you."

She gritted her teeth and snatched up the bucket and the mop. "I don't daydream." She had no idea why she was taking everything out on Clayton. It wasn't his fault that James had killed her ability to dream.

He stepped closer to her and took the mop from her trembling fingers. "What about dreams, Alice?" His fingers tenderly brushed back a wisp of her hair. "Do you dream?"

She met his gaze and was mesmerized by the fascinating fires dancing in the depths of his hazel eyes. Breathlessly she asked, "Dreams?"

"You know the kind." The backs of his fingers trailed down her jaw. "Deep in the night when no one else is around, do you dream?"

"No," she lied. She would never admit to the provocative dreams that had been plaguing her nights since Halloween. Dreams of Clayton. Erotic dreams of tangled sheets, burning needs, and hotter desires. Night after night she had experienced steamy fantasies that she hadn't even known existed until she dreamed them. With every new vision Clayton had accepted the challenge and conquered her desire. A tide of red swept up her face when she remembered the previous night's dream and how Clayton had risen to the erotic challenge.

His fingers followed the flow of red up her cheek. "You're blushing."

She hastily grabbed the mop back out of his hand. "You're mistaken."

He leaned against the archway leading into the kitchen, crossed his arms over his chest, and grinned. "My, my, Miss Alice. I would dearly love to know what is going through that mind of yours right now." His grin grew wider as a deeper red blush flooded her face. "Care to confide in someone? Maybe we could share secrets?"

Murder gleamed in her eyes as she glanced at the damp mop clutched in her fist. She ought to beat him over the head with it. That would wipe that stupid grin off his face. It wasn't her fault she was a terrible liar, it was in her genes. Jorgensens had been speaking their minds for generations, and it went against every strand of her DNA to lie. Clayton was goading her on and didn't deserve to know the truth. A mischievous idea replaced her murderous inclinations. Maybe he did deserve the truth. Maybe if he heard how attracted she was to him, he'd run for the hills and never show his face in

Dodge again. Wasn't he the one who'd said he shouldn't have kissed her first?

Alice leaned the mop handle against the wall and ever so lightly toyed with the bulky knit of Clayton's sweater. Her confidence grew as she felt him stiffen and suck in a harsh breath. He wasn't as relaxed as he would like her to believe. She raised her gaze and smiled. "Do you want to hear every detail, or just an overall description?"

He seemed to stop breathing as she outlined the stitching of his sweater. His back pressed farther into the wood molding. "An overall description will be fine."

"The dreams have only two people in them." Her fingers spread out until both palms were pressed against his chest.

He managed to croak out one word as a light film of sweat broke out across his brow. "Who?"

"Me." Her gaze traveled over every feature of his face. His chin was strong and at times seemed almost arrogant. His nose was a trifle narrow, his cheekbones were high, and his ears were on the large side, but they didn't stick out. His upper lip was thin while his lower lip was full and sexy. It seemed to be begging her to sink her teeth into its softness and taste every essence of his soul. His dark brown hair was a little shaggy, but it was clean and soft and just cried out for her fingers. It was his eyes that captured her attention, though. They seemed to be burning with green-and-gold fire. Hazel fire that was reflecting his building desire.

Her fingers started to tremble against his sweater. Confusion clouded her judgment, and she took a hasty step backward. What was she doing? Telling Clayton about the dreams would be a mistake. He would know exactly what he was doing to her.

He pressed his hands over hers and kept them on his chest. "Who else?"

She blinked and tried to shake off the strange sensation stealing up her arms. It felt like a dozen tiny electrodes of heat were pulsating into her body. "Who else what?"

"Who else was in your dreams?" He pushed away from the doorframe and eliminated any distance between them. "You said there were two people. One was you." His gaze never left her eyes. "Who was the other?"

He wanted her. She could see it in his eyes and feel it in the heavy pounding of his heart beneath her fingers. Clayton wanted to do all those delicious things she had dreamed about. He wasn't promising forever, or even tomorrow, but he was offering her a chance to taste life again. She wanted that chance more than her next breath. She gazed down at her baggy sweater and faded jeans. She did look like a grubby Cinderella before receiving a visit from the fairy godmother. What in the world could he possibly be seeing in her?

She snatched her hands out from under his and took a step backward. "I have to go get ready for dinner." She took another step toward the stairs as his frown deepened. "Maude's expecting us over at George's in a half hour."

She was halfway up the stairs when his voice stopped her. "You didn't answer the question, Alice." He stood at the bottom of the stairs watching her. "Who else was in your dreams?"

She knew he wasn't going to follow her up. They were expected next door in twenty-nine minutes, and they both knew that Maude would come looking for them if they failed to show up. A smile tilted up the corners of her mouth. Clayton was about to be repaid for kissing her senseless in the kitchen. She wanted what was promised in his gaze. She wanted to live again. She watched as his hand gripped the banister ever tighter as he waited for her reply. When she feared damage to the solid oak railing, she gave him what he had been looking for. "You were the other person in those dreams, Clayton."

His harsh groan seemed to echo after her as she continued up the stairs and along the hall to her bedroom.

Clayton swallowed another mouthful of mashed potatoes and swore he was eating paste. His taste buds had gone berserk along with his heart rate and his libido. Alice's declaration that he was the other person in her dreams had left him in a permanent state of semiarousal. That and the fact that she looked sexy as all hell.

He risked another glance across the table at her and paid the price. Heat scorched his gut. For all he knew, he could have been eating jalapeño peppers instead of meat loaf. Alice looked like an angel. When she had joined him in the kitchen fifteen minutes ago, he'd had to use every ounce of his self-control to help her on with her jacket and escort her through the side-yard gate and over to George's. What he really wanted to do was lay her down in a pile of crunchy leaves and make one of his own dreams come true.

Alice had not only changed her clothes, she had taken a shower, washed her hair, and, for the first time he could detect, added the light floral fragrance of perfume. She had put aside her usually baggy sweaters and sweatshirts and was wearing a clinging silk blouse the color of copper, and it reflected the light from the overhead chandelier with every breath she took. Her flowing chiffon skirt swirled around her calves and was printed with a kaleidoscope of fall leaves. She had left her hair long and loose. It cascaded over her shoulders and down her back like a golden waterfall, bewitching him with its silky radiance. Alice looked feminine, delectable, and more mouthwatering than the chocolate cake Maude had baked especially for him.

Clayton forced his gaze back to his plate and pushed around a bunch of string beans with his fork. Who in their right mind could eat while the room temperature had to be pushing ninety-eight? He glanced at Alice's plate and noticed that she wasn't doing much better. Her dainty fingers had been busy using her fork to cut up a large slice of meat loaf into dozens of unappetizing little clumps. It served her right that her appetite was shot too. She never should have told him he was the other person in her dreams, at least not when there wasn't a darn thing he could do about it.

"Are the mashed potatoes okay?" asked Maude, who had been staring oddly at Alice and Clayton all through the meal.

He forced himself to scoop up another forkful. "They're delicious, Maude. It's been a long time since I had honest-to-goodness mashed potatoes, not the instant kind." He popped his fork into his mouth and managed to smile.

Maude frowned at Alice's plate. "What's wrong with the meat loaf? Did I put too many onions in it, or didn't I use enough seasoning?"

Alice guiltily glanced up from cutting a small chunk of meat loaf into a group of meat flakes. "It's perfect, Maude."

"Then why aren't you eating it?"

She shot a quick glance at Clayton before looking back down at her full plate. Her fingers nervously toyed with the handle of her knife.

Clayton watched as Alice opened her mouth to say something, then snapped it shut. She obviously didn't know what to tell Maude. Alice was a terrible liar. He knew why she wasn't eating, it was because of him. If her stomach was tied up in half the knots his was, she had his sympathy. He glanced at Maude and smiled. "I think I can explain." He ignored Alice's sharply indrawn breath. "We celebrated fixing the sink by finishing off the box of cinnamon rolls I bought this morning at the bakery." It wasn't a total lie. They each had had a roll with a glass of milk before cleaning up the kitchen, but it hadn't been enough to spoil their appetites.

"Alice, really," Maude said, amused. "You haven't done anything so naughty in years." She turned to Clayton and grinned. "It must be your influence on her."

"Why my influence?"

"Alice is never naughty." Maude shook her head at her niece. "The worries this girl used to give Herbert and me." She ignored Alice's strangled cries. "She never misbehaved in school, always was on the honor roll, and never missed a curfew." She shared a glance with Herbert. "Do you have any idea what it was like trying to be parents to a perfect child?"

Clayton grinned as Alice grew redder. So Miss-Goody-Two-Shoes was always this way. "Didn't she do anything bad?"

"I wasn't that perfect," Alice exclaimed.

"No, of course not, dear," Maude said. "I remember the time when you were caught stealing apples from old man Bodnar's orchard."

"What happened?" Clayton asked. He couldn't picture Alice stealing from anyone.

"It turned out she was only taking a few apples from a very rich, selfish man and giving them away to a bunch of underprivileged children from town. Her health class had been discussing nutrition and how important it was to eat fruits and vegetables every day."

"I was only thirteen years old," Alice said.

"And has age made you wiser?" Clayton asked.

"Yes." She grinned. "Now I don't get caught."

"Next time you do your apple raid, let me know and I'll drive the getaway car." Somehow it fit Alice to be on the side of the underprivileged children.

"Stop teasing him, Alice, before he thinks you're some kind of criminal." Maude handed Clayton a basket overflowing with warm biscuits. "Bodnar's orchard was bulldozed over seven years ago to make way for that newfangled strip mall those college kids always shop at."

"So how do you make sure the children get their vitamins now?" Clayton asked as he took a biscuit and placed it on his plate. Why in the hell couldn't George own a huge dog, one that lay under the table and had an unquenchable desire for people food? Between Alice's and his plate, they could put five pounds on the dog with just this meal and Maude could stop worrying about why no one was eating her food.

"I write a check," Alice said, sending her aunt a meaningful look.

Maude muttered something that sounded like "among other things" and went back to finishing her dinner.

Clayton pushed the meat loaf around his plate some more, trying to rearrange it to look like he'd eaten more than he had. He didn't want to disappoint Maude, but he couldn't force another forkful down his throat. The only thing he wanted to taste was Alice's sweet, delectable mouth. He glanced over at her and encountered her hungry stare. Yes, she was having the same problem he was. Having dinner with Maude, George, and Herbert was a mistake. He should have kidnapped Alice from the house as soon as she entered the kitchen wearing that incredible outfit and taken her someplace quiet and romantic. Someplace where they could have been alone. Someplace where he could have pried her dreams out of her and seen if they matched his own.

With an abrupt movement Clayton stood up. "I forgot." If he didn't get Alice out of the room immediately, he was going to do something drastic. Like kiss her in front of everyone.

"Forgot what?" George asked.

"I have to pick up something before the store closes."

"What?" Maude asked.

"Ah . . ." Clayton looked at Alice. She shrugged. No help there. "Ah . . ." He glanced around the formal dining room that looked so much like Maude's. He spotted George's television in the other room with a VCR sitting on top. "Videos!" He smiled at Maude. "I promised myself that I would rent some movies and catch up on what I've been missing by working so late."

"Well, of course, dear," Maude said. "You run on out and get those movies. We have a VCR hooked up in the family room." She smiled at her niece. "Why don't you go with him, Alice? You have such good taste in films."

Alice was out of her chair and halfway across the room before she remembered the mess sitting on the table. "I really should stay and help clean up." The words seemed to be dragged from her.

"Nonsense, dear," her aunt said. "You helped Clayton fix the sink. We can handle a few dirty dishes. Besides, George's dishwasher is even bigger than ours."

Alice glanced at Clayton, who nodded. He helped her on with her coat and quickly jammed his own arms into the sleeves of his jacket. They were both outside before Maude, George, and Herbert's good-byes faded.

He grabbed her hand and pulled her through the front yard, away from the windows and any prying eyes.

He headed for a huge maple tree that was in its last stages of losing its multicolored leaves. Backing her against the thick trunk, he covered her mouth with his, giving the kiss that had been burning on his lips all through dinner.

SIX

Alice wrapped her arms around Clayton's neck and savored the kiss she had been dying for since he'd caught her daydreaming in the hallway. The only thing that kept her from falling into a mass of sensual delight at his feet was the solid tree pressed against her back and Clayton's arms.

She had been thinking about this kiss all evening. This was the kiss that was going to allow her to taste life again. While showering, she'd concluded that maybe Maude had been right all along, she had been hiding from life. There were no rules that said a person had to have dreams to live. Why shouldn't she accept Clayton for what he was, a sexy, handsome, caring, and intelligent man? Her heart and head both knew he would only be staying for a short time. Whom would it hurt? Her decision to further a relationship with Clayton came from reality, not dreams.

She parted her lips beneath his searching tongue and

threaded her fingers into his hair. A low moan rumbled in the back of her throat as their tongues did an erotic dance together. He tasted of seductive pleasures and indecent proposals too good to pass up. It had been a long time since she had been with a man, or had wanted a man as much as she wanted Clayton.

She felt her nipples bud into tight, hard peaks under the delicate lace of her bra. The liquid heat pooling at the junction of her thighs seemed to be flowing from every pore of her body. Desires that had been suppressed for years awakened and burned out of control. She had been mistaken. She had never wanted another man as much as she wanted Clayton this very minute. With one kiss he had inflamed a hunger she never knew she possessed. In retaliation for this overwhelming craving she nipped at his moist lower lip.

Clayton groaned in pleasure and released her mouth. His lips nuzzled her throat as he tried to catch his breath. The tip of his tongue traced the wildly beating vein in her neck. He growled, "Do you have any idea what you're doing to me?"

She leaned her head against the rough bark of the tree and tried to capture her hair, which the wind was blowing around her face. "Is it the same thing that you're doing to me?"

His lips nuzzled the sensitive area behind her ear before dipping down to lavish the same treatment on the silky skin beneath the collar of her blouse and coat. His hands slid down her back and cupped her bottom, bringing her up against his obvious arousal. "What am I doing to you?"

She sighed and felt herself melt against him. He was definitely feeling the same overpowering sensations. "I feel like a marshmallow that stepped too close to a flame."

His rich chuckle was muffled against the collar of her coat. "You're right on both accounts. I am burning up, and a marshmallow is pure sugar." He raised his head and brushed back a long strand of golden hair that the wind was whipping across her face. "What do you suggest we do about that?"

"If we had some chocolate and graham crackers, we could make a s'more." She knew exactly what she wanted to do with her marshmallow and his flame, and making s'mores wasn't on her list. Unless she could somehow entice him into some more. . . .

He brushed a kiss across her cheek. "Food wasn't exactly what I had in mind."

She released her wind-whipped hair and jammed her freezing hands into her coat pockets. Now that he'd stopped kissing her, she could feel the cold northern wind, see the colorful leaves dancing in the currents, and smell the burning wood from distant woodstoves. It was a perfect night to take a lover home and snuggle with him under the quilts. "What did you have in mind?"

Clayton glanced at the house behind him where Maude, Herbert, and George were. He turned his gaze to the house in front of them, an empty house that wouldn't be empty for long. Stepping away from her, he allowed the brisk wind to cool their bodies.

"Videos," he said. "Herbert and Maude will be expecting to see a stack of movies when they come home."

Alice glanced at her house and frowned. How could she have forgotten about her aunt and uncle? Maude would have heart failure and poor Herbie would have to haul down the antique musket from over the mantel in the family room if they came home and found her in bed with Clayton. Great! She finally decided to start living again, only to discover she had about as much freedom as a schoolgirl. Why in the world hadn't she moved out of the house years ago? She studied Clayton's brown leather loafers that were half buried beneath red and orange dried leaves. She hadn't moved out because Maude and Herbert were her responsibility. They depended on her.

Maybe it was better to call a halt to this silly infatuation with Clayton now, before things got out of hand. Sneaking up and down the upstairs hallway playing musical beds in the middle of the night didn't strike her as romantic. It had more of a feel of desperation to it.

She ran her gaze up Clayton's brown twill pants and thick cable-knit sweater. The brown leather jacket he had on looked comfortable and well worn. In the thin light of dusk she couldn't read his expression, but she did notice that his posture seemed awfully tense. Before she could stop herself, her hand reached out and caressed the side of his face. He had shaved earlier, and his clenched jaw felt like it was made out of granite. He hadn't wanted to stop either, but he had.

"There's a video store in the mall by the university," she said.

He turned his head and pressed a kiss into the center of her palm. A shiver raced through her as his tongue caressed her heart line. He grabbed her hand and started to drag her around the front of the house to where his car was parked.

"Just keep reminding me," he said, "videos, videos, videos." His voice continued in a low, raspy murmur as he led the way over the slate walk. "And we just might make it to the store tonight."

Clayton picked up another video and frowned. "Don't they make movies anymore without sex?" It was the fifth movie he'd selected that was rated R because of nudity. The one thing he didn't want to do that night was sit in the same room as Alice and watch someone else make love. His body could only withstand so much punishment in one evening. Being in the same room as Alice without touching her was going to be punishment enough.

He jammed the video back onto the shelf and picked up the one next to it. The front cover showed some space alien tearing its way out of a poor person's gut. He slid it back into its place with a shudder.

Alice came up beside him. "I found one that seems to fit all your requirements: a new release, no sex, no graphic violence, and no unnecessary profanity." A smile teased her mouth as she handed him the video.

He glanced down at it and couldn't help smiling himself. Alice had selected Disney's latest animated film. "Am I that bad?"

"No." She took the tape from him and placed it back

on its cardboard display. "You don't have to worry about offending Maude and Herbert."

He glanced at the assortment of new releases. "Do they usually watch these kinds of movies?"

"Maude likes to go to bed early, so she won't even start to watch a movie unless you put it on right after the evening news."

He glanced at his watch and grinned. The evening news was over an hour ago. "That takes care of Maude. What about Herbert?"

"I have never known my uncle to stay awake past the opening credits." She picked a video off the shelf and handed it to him. "This one is great if you like westerns." Another video was plucked from the shelf. "This one is a little on the racy side, but I heard the mystery is masterful." She toyed with her lower lip as she scanned the titles. "This one is supposedly hilarious, and this one is a 'must see' adventure."

Clayton balanced the stack of growing videos. "Have you seen all of these?" He wanted Alice to enjoy the movies, too, not just sit through them. If he hadn't used such a lame excuse to leave dinner early, he could have taken her to the movies that night. At least then he could have had her all to himself for a couple of hours.

"Oh, I haven't seen any of those," she said. She continued to scan the rack.

"Then how do you know if they're any good?"

"I read reviews." A smile lit up her face as she spotted another video. She added it to the pile.

He glanced down at the picture of an actor who had been proclaimed the sexiest man in America by a national magazine for the fourth year in a row. The actor looked rugged, dangerous, and, if you were into blue eyes and chiseled jaws, sexy. "And what does this movie have about it that makes it worth viewing?" Clayton asked. He already knew the answer, but he wanted to tease Alice.

She grinned and pointed to the review printed on the front cover. "See? It was given 'two thumbs up.'"

Clayton chuckled and headed for the register. "Come on, let's get out of here before you add any more to this pile."

"You're renting all of them?"

He handed the stack of tapes to the teenager with spiked hair behind the counter. "It's supposed to rain all day tomorrow." His gaze caught and held hers. "Can you think of something better to do on rainy days?" He knew exactly how *he* wanted to spend a rainy Sunday: underneath his quilt making love to Alice over and over again.

Alice was the first to break the heated glance. She nervously fidgeted with the buttons on her coat. "No. Watching movies sure beats endless hours of Sunday football games."

Clayton grumbled incoherently, yawned loudly, and stumbled his way to the bathroom like a blind man. He had done the unimaginable, he had overslept. It was after ten o'clock. He didn't have anywhere or anything to do on this cold and raining Sunday, but wasting the morning away in bed was unthinkable. Especially since he had been alone. Alice, the sexy angel who tormented his dreams, was somewhere downstairs. He needed to see if her mouth was as incredibly delicious as he remembered. He hadn't had a chance to taste its sweetness since they had stood under the maple tree in George's yard.

It was all Herbert's fault. The man should have been asleep the first twenty minutes of the movie last night, just like Alice had said. But no, Herbert had had at least three naps yesterday. One had even lasted the final three-quarters of the Notre Dame football game. For two cents Clayton would march over to George's house and set his comfortable leather recliner on fire. If Herbert hadn't gotten those extra hours of sleep, Clayton would have had Alice to himself last night, instead of having to share her with a seventy-two-year-old man. After watching only one movie, the western Herbert had picked out, everyone had called it a night.

Clayton muttered something dangerous as he stepped under the hot shower and allowed the stinging spray to jolt him awake. The night had seemed like an eternity. He had tossed and turned. He had tried to read three different books. He had studied every faded photo hanging on the walls at least a dozen times. He had even gone so far as to sneak downstairs and fix himself a cup of warm milk after his search for something stronger proved futile. His only saving grace was he didn't have to pass Alice's bedroom to get downstairs. He really hadn't known if he had the strength to walk by knowing she was only a couple feet away snuggled under a warm quilt.

He stepped from the shower and vigorously rubbed

his body with a fluffy dark blue towel. He needed to get downstairs and find Alice before she managed to slip away from him again. Tonight, somehow, they were going to be alone. Even if he had to resort to putting knockout drops in Herbert's after-dinner tea.

He finished dressing and stepped out into the hall. The only sound he could detect was the faint ticking of the grandfather clock in the downstairs hall. He descended the stairs and headed for the kitchen, where he hoped to find Alice.

He halted outside the kitchen when he heard Alice and Maude talking. Once again his hopes of finding Alice alone went sliding down the tubes. So much for any good-morning kisses. He took a deep breath, plastered on a friendly smile, and entered the room.

"Of course you're going," Alice was saying.

Maude shook her head and played with the handle on her teacup. "But that would leave you handling everything here."

"Don't worry about us. Herbert and I will be fine." Alice squeezed her aunt's hand. "Your sister needs you, Maude. You have to go."

"I want to help her, but I don't want to dump everything on your shoulders." Maude dabbed at the moisture gathering in her eyes with a lacy white handkerchief. "What about Clayton? I can't expect you to take care of him too."

"What about me?" Clayton walked farther into the room and studied the two women. Maude looked pale and upset, while Alice looked determined.

"Maude's sister, Martha, fell last night and broke her

hip," Alice explained. "The hospital won't keep her more than a few days if she has someone at home to look after her. Martha called this morning and asked Maude to come stay with her for a couple of weeks, since her own children have to work and have their own families to care for. Martha doesn't want to go live with any of them. She'd be much more comfortable in her own home."

"I'm sorry to hear about your sister, Maude. But what does that have to do with me?" Clayton asked.

Maude sniffled. "Alice wants me to go."

"I agree," he said. He sat down next to her and patted the back of her trembling hand. "I'm sure your sister is receiving the best medical treatment, and the fact that it was she who called you should make you feel better."

"It does," Maude said. "But how can I go and leave poor Alice to handle everything here?" She returned Clayton's act of kindness by squeezing his hand. "I can't expect her to work all day and come home to a house that needs cleaning and meals that need cooking."

Alice chuckled. "Millions of women do it every day, Maude. We'll be fine, I promise."

"Millions of women don't take in boarders," Maude said.

"Ah. . . . Now I get it," Clayton said. "Would it make you feel better if I moved out?" It was the answer to his dilemma. With Maude gone, he would still have Herbert under foot. Granted he wouldn't be able to see Alice as much, but if he moved out, he would at least have someplace they could be alone together. He turned his head and gazed at Alice. A spark of hope leaped inside him. She looked like she didn't relish the idea of him moving out.

"I can't ask you to leave!" Maude exclaimed.

"Of course he's not leaving," Alice said. She glared at Clayton for upsetting her aunt. "I'm sure he won't mind take out food a couple times a week, would you, Clayton?"

He'd eat cardboard sandwiches and plastic fruit if Alice was the one serving them. "I'll even volunteer to be the one to run out and get it." So much for his fantasy of getting Alice alone in this century.

"See, Maude, everything here will be fine. You just worry about packing and making Martha comfortable. I'll call the airlines and see about getting you a flight to Baltimore."

Maude dabbed at her eyes again. "Promise that you'll call me if you need me back here?"

"We always need you here, Maude. You should know that." Alice leaned across the table and kissed her aunt's cheek. "Your sister is the one who needs you now. Go to her. I'm sure we can all manage for a few weeks on my cooking." She stood up and headed for the phone. "After all, I did have the best cook in Harper County to teach me."

Five minutes later Alice had just finished making Maude's reservation for a flight the next morning, when George came strolling through the back door on the pretense of getting a slice of Maude's chocolate cake. Alice chuckled at his obvious ploy. She and Herbert hadn't been wrong about George's feelings toward Maude. Between her aunt, Clayton, and herself, they explained to George how Maude was heading east for a few weeks to care for her sister. Alice's mouth fell open when George announced that he refused to allow Maude to travel to Baltimore alone. He would accompany her.

Clayton and Alice both observed the stubborn streak George was displaying and backed out of the argument. Alice was pleased that her aunt wouldn't be traveling alone and was secretly overjoyed at the blush stealing up Maude's cheeks. She wasn't as immune to their next-door neighbor as she would like everyone to believe.

Maude had just lost the argument and was graciously accepting George's assistance, when Herbert, who had just awakened from his morning nap, ambled into the kitchen. He took one look around the crowded room and demanded to know what was going on.

Clayton and Alice leaned against the counter and watched as George and Maude stumbled their way through an explanation of why they were leaving together tomorrow for Baltimore. Herbert listened to the explanation with a deepening frown. When Maude finished the story, he calmly folded his arms across his chest and said, "I'm going too."

"What?" George exclaimed.

Alice tried to hide her smile as Maude, Herbert, and George began arguing. Within five minutes the whole thing was settled. All three would be flying to Baltimore the next morning.

Alice juggled the two shopping bags into her one arm and popped the mail between her teeth while trying to insert the key into the back door. She jammed her hip against the wooden frame to stop the hazardous slide of the bag with the two dozen eggs on top. The key finally slipped into the lock just as she felt her pantyhose snag on the doorframe. The door swung open, she reshifted the bags and her purse, and made a mad dash for the counter. The bags safely landed on the counter as a tingly sensation raced up her leg. With an impatient gesture she yanked the mail from her mouth and glared down at the offending runner that went from mid-calf to the waistband. *What else could possibly go wrong?*

She glanced around the kitchen and sighed. The breakfast dishes were still scattered on the table and in the sink. The morning hadn't gone as smoothly as she would have liked, but she had managed to get Maude, Herbert, and George to the airport within fourteen minutes of their departure time. Alice couldn't tell if Maude was more distressed about leaving her alone with their boarder to care for or the fact that she had to leave with dirty dishes still on the table. All the way to the airport Herbert had swung from going to not going. He couldn't figure out which one of the Jorgensen females needed his protection the most or, more accurately, which suitor he trusted the least—George, who was dropping everything to accompany Maude, or the nice doctor who fixed the leaky sink. In the end he flipped a coin, it came up tails, and he got on the plane with Maude and George. From those chaotic beginnings the day had managed to get progressively worse.

She had walked into work an hour late, only to discover that both of her assistants had called in sick with the flu. Before lunch she'd had five urgent requests from various professors, had to take a group of financial supporters on a tour of the library, and the computers had gone down. Clayton had called sometime after one while she was sitting at her desk reading some inane article on fungicides and eating a container of vanilla yogurt. As she started to put away the groceries, she remembered the feelings that had washed over her when she had heard Clayton's voice on the phone. He had sounded as if he had just awakened and was still lying in bed. A tantalizing vision flashed in her mind. Her fingers trembled so badly, she dropped one of the eggs she was trying to place in the egg holder in the refrigerator door. The gooey yoke and white splattered all over her shoe and lower leg.

She muttered a few choice words concerning raspy male voices and eggs as she mopped up the mess with a handful of paper towels. All he done was ask if she had gotten everyone off safely and to tell her he wouldn't be home until sometime after six. Nothing to get so flustered about. He hadn't done anything that other boarders hadn't done before. He was being a perfect gentleman.

So why did her heart tell her something different? Why was there something in his voice that wasn't quite boarderlike?

Alice glanced at the clock and groaned. It was a quarter to six. With the way her luck was going, Clayton would be strolling through the front door any minute now. Against all odds her afternoon had been worse than the morning. Why in the hell hadn't she agreed with

Clayton when he offered to pick up something on his way home? Here he was being nice and thoughtful, and she blew it by trying to be superwoman.

Ever since she'd realized what it could mean, them having the house to themselves for weeks, her imagination had been working overtime. Last night she had lain in bed thinking up recipes with which she could dazzle him with her culinary skills. She had also done a mental inventory of her lingerie drawer. By two o'clock in the morning she was praying for a Victoria's Secret catalog and the courage to wear some of their clothes.

She took off her navy suit jacket and dropped it onto the back of a chair. As she kicked her sticky shoes into the corner, she rolled up the sleeves of her white silk blouse. With any luck she could whip together something and have it in the oven before Clayton got home. She opened the dishwasher and started to jam the dirty breakfast dishes into it. Someone had left coffee in the bottom of his cup. It ended up on the front of her skirt. She reached for the dishrag and the faucet to wipe the stain before it set, and ended up spraying cold water onto her blouse. With a frustrated curse she tossed the rag back into the sink, unbuttoned the top two buttons on her blouse, and pulled the soaking material away from her chest.

Tears blurred her vision as she glanced around the room. It was in shambles. She was in shambles. She had been in charge for only ten hours, and already she had trashed Maude's immaculate kitchen, dinner was going to be late, if at all, and she had gotten lipstick stains all over one of Clayton's letters when she'd jammed the mail into her mouth to free up her hands. Her day had gone from bad to the worst. With the back of her hand she rubbed her eyes and tried to stick a lock of hair that had escaped the bun back into place. She only succeeded in making the entire bun slip past the collar of her blouse to hang drunkenly between her shoulder blades.

Her nerves were shot and her body was frustrated. Two nights with barely a few hours of sleep between them were taking their toll. She couldn't think straight. What had happened to the mental shopping list she had compiled around midnight? She had entered the grocery store and her mind had gone blank. She couldn't remember one darn meal she had coordinated with such delight. She had ended up buying the basics and praying something would come to her on the drive home. As it stood right this minute, she was either ordering pizza or Clayton would be dining on Hamburger Helper.

She closed the dishwasher. How could she possibly think about dinner when one question overruled her mind and confiscated her every thought? *Was Clayton going to be her lover tonight?* She knew he wanted to, and if she was honest with herself, she felt the same way. But that didn't mean they would become lovers. She glanced down at herself and sighed. Who in his right mind would want to become her lover? Her hair was a mess and her eyes were puffy from lack of sleep. Her white silk blouse was soaked and splattered with tiny brown specks. A coffee stain marked the front of her skirt, one leg was covered in dried egg yolk, while the other boasted a runner the size of the Continental Railroad.

She needed a shower more than Clayton needed a

home-cooked meal. With a purposeful stride, she marched over to a drawer and yanked out the phone book. After flipping a couple of pages she found what she was looking for, picked up the phone, and punched out seven numbers.

A moment later she said, "Yes, this is Alice Jorgensen. I would like to order a large pizza."

After completing her call, she slowly replaced the receiver and shook her head at the room. It would just have to wait. First thing she needed was a shower and a change of clothes before Clayton got home. Then she would see about tackling the kitchen and whipping up a salad to go along with the pizza.

She picked up her jacket and her sticky shoes and headed down the hall toward the stairs. If Clayton came home from work now and saw her like this, he would run in terror. She wasn't an expert on seduction, but dried egg yolk didn't seem like a turn-on to her.

She passed the grandfather clock and was at the bottom of the stairs when the front door opened. She closed her eyes in embarrassment as Clayton stepped into the hall. Her day had finally hit rock bottom. What else could possibly go wrong? Preparing herself for the look of revulsion that surely must be on his face, she opened her eyes.

His smile was the first thing she noticed. Confused, she raised her gaze and encountered the same smile dancing in his eyes. A smile and desire. She could see the heat he was trying to hide behind the smile. Clayton wanted her!

Her shoes fell to the floor as he stepped forward and handed her a single white rose.

His smile broadened to a grin as his gaze skimmed down her body, from her disarrayed hair to her bare feet. His voice was light with amusement as he said, "Hi, honey, I'm home."

SEVEN

If he wasn't standing there looking at Alice, Clayton would never have believed it. She was frazzled and rumpled and incredibly sexy. She looked like she had suffered through the same kind of day he'd had. Only she looked a little worse for wear. Lord how he'd missed her. He had only spent one weekend in her company doing no more than sharing a few heated kisses and already he had felt lost without her. What was going to happen when they became lovers?

He noticed that the rose she clutched in her fingers was trembling. His grin faded to a smile of sympathy. She looked like she could use a hug. "Is this the time when I should ask you 'How was your day?'"

She toyed with the stem of the rose and blinked back a wave of tears. "There aren't enough hours left in the day for me to tell you how rotten my day was." She raised the bloom to her nose and sniffed. Over the top of the white petals her moist gaze encountered his. "Thank you. I think you just turned it around."

He should have brought her an entire dozen instead of the lone flower. But he had thought a single white rose would make a more powerful statement than an entire bouquet of red ones. He looked down at the single rose. "It looks lonely, doesn't it?"

She studied the flower for a moment, then a wondrous smile curved her mouth. "No, Clayton, it looks beautiful."

He knew neither one of them was talking about the rose. He took a step closer and brushed back a wayward lock of her hair. Golden silk ran through his fingers. "So do you."

She chuckled and shook her head. "Did you lose your contacts now?"

"No, they're in." He stroked the soft curve of her cheek, his thumb gently caressing the shadows under her eyes. Her sleepless nights were as telling as his. His gaze roamed her face. She was beautiful. From her wide blue eyes to her generous mouth that always seemed to be begging for his kisses. Kisses he was now free to give her without anyone interrupting. He leaned forward and brushed his lips over hers.

"Is this your way of asking what's for dinner?" Her gaze was fastened hungrily on his mouth.

Clayton swallowed hard and took a step back. If she continued to look at him like that, neither one of them was going to eat dinner. The only thing he could smell was her intoxicating scent, the potent mixture of her shampoo, and some elusive fragrance that could only be described as Alice. No aroma of cooking food teased his senses. She obviously hadn't had time to start dinner yet.

He cleared his throat. "Do you want to go out and get something to eat, or would you rather I go pick us up something?"

She gave him a funny smile. "Do you like pizza?"

"I love it. I could eat it seven nights a week." Which was basically what he had been doing before he moved in there.

"Great. It should be here in about twenty minutes." With an impish grin she backed toward the steps. "Pay the man when he gets here." She started to climb the stairs. "The money's on the kitchen table."

Clayton chuckled as she disappeared up the steps and out of sight. That's what he got for begging off work early for the first time in his life. The team had placed its order for pizza and with knowing smiles had practically shoved him out the door. He hadn't been much help that day. Twice he had been caught daydreaming. He'd known he was out of it when Richard Stomer had glanced over his shoulder and made a comment on his doodling. Dr. Clayton Williams had been caught doodling? What in the hell was the world coming to? He never doodled and he never once left work before the rest of the team. What was Alice doing to him? Not only had he spent the day fantasizing about her delectable body, but he'd actually thought about her smile and the warm feeling that crept into his heart whenever she entered a room.

His gaze stayed on the top of the stairs where Alice had just been. An astounding thought struck him, and he gripped the newel. He was falling in love! It was the only explanation. He had experienced chemistry, lust, and desire before, but this was different. Alice was pulling at all those emotions and more. Much more. Emotions that connected Alice to the rest of his life and his future happiness. A smart man would run for the hills, and wasn't he considered a smart man? Didn't he have the I.Q. and degrees to prove it? So why was he standing there with his heart in his hand and, instead of figuring out a way to put it back into his chest, wondering how to get Alice to accept it?

Alice's feet halted as soon as she entered the kitchen thirty minutes later. It was immaculate and empty. *Where was Clayton?* She heard a sound coming from the dining room and headed in that direction. A smile curved her mouth when she spotted the dining-room table. Clayton had set the table for two with Maude's finest china. Two white tapered candles gave off the only light. A crystal bowl was overflowing with a freshly made salad. Her glance found the man responsible for the transformation. He was standing by the buffet carefully placing a slice of steaming pizza on each of their plates before carrying them over to the table.

He gallantly held out her chair. "Your dinner awaits."

She sat down and smiled as he handed her a linen napkin. "Thank you." *A person could get used to coming home after a hard day at work to this kind of treatment,* she mused. Soft music was coming from the family room, where Clayton had obviously found Herbert's jazz collection. Candlelight gleamed off the crystal glasses, and the pizza smelled heavenly. If Clayton was planning a seduction, the only thing missing was the wine.

"I'm sorry," he said, seeming to read her thoughts, "but you only have a choice of lite beer, grape juice, or soda. I can't seem to find any wine, but I did manage to locate a bottle of cooking sherry."

Alice bit her lower lip to keep from chuckling. So much for the seduction routine. "Soda will be fine. Maude doesn't keep any alcohol around because of Herbert. After he returned from overseas, he . . . How shall I put it? His best friend was the bottom of the bottle."

"Does the friendship still exist?" He popped the top of a can of soda and poured it into her glass.

"No, but Maude doesn't believe in tempting fate." She took the glass Clayton handed her and grinned. There was something uniquely different about drinking soda out of Waterford crystal.

Clayton filled his own glass and sat down. "I'd like to propose a toast."

"To what?" She raised her glass and studied the strange gleam that had entered his eyes. What in the world was he thinking?

"To us," he whispered. He held his glass out toward hers.

Alice swallowed the heavy knot of desire clogging her throat. She now knew what he had been thinking. The same thing she had been pondering all weekend, making love. It was in the way he was looking at her, all hot and steamy. It was in the hushed music, the crystal, and the soft glow of the candlelight. Clayton was on the same wavelength as she. A nervous smile flitted across her mouth. Tonight she was going to live out one of those dreams that had been plaguing her since Clayton arrived. She and Clayton were about to become lovers.

She touched her glass to his. "To us."

Clayton entered the family room and groaned. He knew he had taken too long. His expression softened as he looked down at Alice asleep on the couch. It was his own fault. After dinner he had insisted that she sit on the couch and listen to the music while he lit a fire. After he'd gotten a cheerful blaze going, he'd returned to the kitchen and cleaned up. Alice had one hell of a day, and he'd wanted her to relax and enjoy their first evening together. After the dishwasher had been loaded and the dining room put back in order, he had dashed upstairs to take a shower.

He rubbed his smooth jaw, then quietly added another log to the fire. So much for the extra five minutes it had taken him to shave. It looked like Alice's delicate skin wouldn't be appreciating his efforts that night. He sat back on his heels and jabbed at the burning logs. *Patience!* When had he lost the ability to be patient?

He glanced over his shoulder at the woman curled up on the couch, dead to the world. She looked like a golden-haired angel, all softness and light. She had joined him for dinner wearing an ivory-colored blouse that reminded him of a man's tuxedo shirt. The rows of ruffles that ran down the front of the shirt had drawn his attention to her breasts all through the meal. Her tailored pants were a light beige, and a gold belt glittered around her tiny waist. Alice had gone from prudish schoolmarm to provocative angel in the space of thirty minutes. Now she was a provocative sleeping angel.

He rose to his feet and stretched before sitting in the same chair as the other night. He had a wonderful view of either Alice or the lively flames as they burned around the logs. He chose Alice, the sleeping angel, the woman he was falling in love with. The woman who could fulfill his dreams of a family and a home of his own. He never realized how desperately he had been dreaming about a family until Alice had entered his life. His gaze softened as it caressed the woman sleeping in the golden glow of the firelight.

What made people fall in love with each other? he wondered. Was it their appearance? The way they acted? The way they talked? Or were you born with it, part of your DNA? Maybe he should resign from the team working on teleportation and start his own research project; falling in love. If he could pinpoint exactly what made a person fall in love and enhance it, the possibilities would be endless. He could originate world peace. Clayton chuckled as he envisioned himself standing on a podium accepting the Nobel Peace Prize. And all because of Alice and the effect she had on the three big *H*s; his hormones, his heart, and his head.

The raging hormones he understood. This was the same chemical substance that had occasionally slipped out of control since his fifteenth birthday. Since he'd met Alice, his body had been producing the chemical substance twenty-four hours a day.

His heart was an entirely different story. The strain Alice was putting on the old ticker was lethal. One minute it was beating away calmly, minding its own business, and bam, Alice walked into view. Instant gallop. When he thought about kissing her, the gallop turned into a thunderous jackhammer; and the feel of her mouth under his sent his blood flying through the heart so fast, there wasn't time to replenish any of the oxygen. That would explain the light-headedness and trembling he felt every time he kissed her. Twice even, when he'd gazed into her eyes, he would swear the damn organ had stopped beating altogether. Her slightest smile squeezed it and her laughter lightened it. No woman had ever affected it that way before.

It was her effect on his mind that was causing him the most problems. How was he supposed to concentrate at work when all he thought about was Alice and her scrumptious kisses? No woman had ever crossed the line between desire and his work before, and he wasn't sure how to handle it.

He stretched his legs out in front of him and shifted his bottom forward. His head naturally found the comfortable corner between the back of the wing chair and its side. He saw a smile play peekaboo with one corner of Alice's mouth and wondered what she was dreaming.

Love was a complicated emotion. His heart was telling him to be quiet and allow Alice to catch up on some much-needed sleep. His howling hormones were crying for him to wake her up with long, hot kisses, declare his feelings, then carry her upstairs and show her exactly how much he loved her. His mind was screaming, *Cau-*

tion! He should slow down and give her the time she needed to catch up with him. It had taken thirty-four years for love to find him, and he didn't want to scare Alice away by moving too quickly. Maybe he had misinterpreted the heated glances she'd shot his way during dinner. This was their first night alone in the house. Maude and Herbert would be away for weeks. Time was on his side.

Clayton sighed heavily, closed his eyes, and willed his body to behave. Patience! He must remember to have patience. Didn't good things come to those who waited? Making love to Alice was going to be good, so very good.

Alice slowly opened her eyes and glanced around the dimly lit room. She had done it again, fallen asleep. Clayton must think she was as bad as Herbert, napping all the time. She glanced at the man sitting near the fireplace and smiled as she sat up. Clayton was asleep too!

She stood and stretched the kinks out of her back. He looked adorable asleep. His lips were slightly parted and his hair was all mussed from leaning against the side of the chair. She resisted the urge to run her fingers through the silky hair and kiss those inviting lips. The poor man had to be dead on his feet to fall asleep in that uncomfortable chair. It was great for reading, and even watching television, but sleeping? No way. At least she had crashed on the couch. His face was out of the glow of the fire, but she could still visualize the heavy shadows under his eyes that she had noticed during dinner. Clayton was suffering from her own ailment, sleepless nights. Was he the one she kept hearing go downstairs into the kitchen at all hours of the night?

She glanced at the clock on the VCR. It was barely after nine. If Clayton had cleaned up the dinner dishes and taken a shower, as his change of clothes suggested, then he couldn't have been asleep for more than half an hour. She never should have agreed to his suggestion that he handle the dinner mess if she did breakfast. He was Maude's boarder, and he was paying extra for cooked meals and hassle-free living. Not the other way around. She had noticed earlier that the money she had left on the kitchen table to pay for the pizza was still there. Not only had he served and cleaned up dinner, but he had paid for it as well.

While he had been busy playing galley slave, she had been sitting with her feet up in front of a roaring fire fantasizing. It didn't matter that she had been fantasizing about Clayton. She seemed to be doing that constantly, and it only added to her frustration. Even worse, every hour in Clayton's company added to that growing mound of frustration too. She needed a release. A release only Clayton could give her.

For one brief second she'd nearly cheered when she'd found out Maude and Herbert would be flying to Baltimore. She'd been distressed to hear about Aunt Martha's fall and her subsequent lengthy recuperation, but to have Clayton all to herself was going to be ecstasy. At least she'd thought so during dinner. He was attentive, showed a wonderful sense of humor, and was devastatingly sexy. She hadn't realized just how potent his charm was until he turned it on full force. What woman could resist a man who hung on her every word, caused her heart to stop beating with just a smile, and insisted on cleaning up? Not her. She'd wanted Clayton since Saturday night when he'd kissed her under George's maple tree.

She glanced between the dying fire and Clayton's handsome face and sighed. Tonight wasn't going to be the night they become lovers. She had to have patience. They would have weeks alone together. She rubbed her arms against the growing chill in the room. Patience was the key.

Very carefully she stepped over his outstretched legs and picked up a log from the basket near the hearth. She knelt down and placed it on top of the red embers. It would have been easier to turn up the thermostat, but she liked watching Clayton sleep in the firelight. She used the poker to position the log more securely. Dancing orange flames leaped and crackled around the dried bark.

"You look like an angel kneeling there."

She whipped her head around. Clayton was awake and watching her. Golden light from the blazing fire bathed his face. "You're awake."

"Either that or I'm dreaming again."

She couldn't tell if his voice was so husky from sleep or from desire. She prayed it was the latter. "Again?"

"I seem to have this recurring dream about you and firelight." His body stayed motionless and his eyes remained uncertain, as if he wasn't sure if he really was awake or dreaming.

Alice watched the way his gaze darkened and reflected the flames dancing behind her. The fire seemed to be coming directly from his soul. She toyed with the brass handle of the poker. "Want to tell me about it?"

He considered the question an awfully long time. "You're standing in front of a fire," he said at last.

"This fire?"

"I'm not sure. All I know is that there's a fire in the background bathing you in golden light." He gripped the arms of the chair. "Your hair is loose and flowing. It seems alive with a thousand golden lights. There's almost a halo effect surrounding your head, just like it is now." His voice trailed off in wonder.

Alice swallowed twice, trying to bring some moisture back into her suddenly dry mouth. "What was I doing?"

Clayton's fingers turned white against the chair arms. "You were standing there smiling at me."

"That's all?"

"No."

She waited endless moments for him to continue. He didn't. It wasn't fair, he couldn't leave the story there. She needed to know what he had been dreaming. For some reason it was vitally important to find out. "Tell me what I was doing, Clayton."

His gaze dropped to her breasts for an instant before jerking back up to her face. The flames burning in his eyes had nothing to do with the fire behind her. "You were taking off your blouse."

She wet her dry lips and felt her breathing quicken. "What did I do with it?"

"You dropped it to the floor, along with your bra."

"Is that all?" Her voice cracked with desire. She could feel her breasts swell and her nipples harden. How could he possibly excite her so much without touching her, without kissing her? The man was five feet away from her and she was melting.

"No, sweet Alice," he growled. "You stood there and tortured me out of my mind as you slowly removed every stitch of clothing from your gorgeous body. The reflection of the flames danced across your skin like a lover's caress, begging me to follow."

"And did you follow?" she asked, breathless.

He groaned and closed his eyes. "I don't know." He leaned his head back wearily. "I keep waking up."

Alice remained kneeling on the floor surrounded by frustration. He had pulled her into his fantasy and left her hanging. She wanted him to continue. She wanted him to teach her how to live again. To have Clayton as a lover, if only for a brief time, would be tasting life again. She knew there would never be a *forever* in this affair with Clayton. He would be leaving when the project he was working on was finished, and she would be staying here with Maude, Herbert, and the university's library. But they could have this time together. She could give Clayton his dream of firelight, and she could taste life.

With fingers that trembled she slowly replaced the poker and stood up. Her knees were weak and her heart was thundering against her rib cage. She glanced at Clayton. He still had his eyes closed and looked to be in utter misery. She took a deep breath, smiled, and reached for the top button on her blouse.

Clayton opened his eyes when he didn't hear Alice storm from the room. His startled gaze followed her fingers as she undid the third button on her blouse. "What are you doing?" he asked.

Her fingers fumbled with the next button. "What does it look like I'm doing?"

"Unbuttoning your blouse," he snapped.

She chuckled. "Glad to see they don't pass out all those fancy degrees to just anybody." She pulled the blouse from the waistband of her pants and undid the last button.

His gaze was riveted to the small gap running down the center of her chest. He could barely make out the white of her bra. "I know what you're doing. What I want to know is why."

She undid the buttons on each cuff. "Why do you think?" The ivory blouse landed near her feet.

He shook his head. "I don't even want to hazard a guess."

She undid the narrow gold belt and pulled it through the loops of her pants. It landed on top of the blouse. She could feel the heat from the fire warming her back, but it was the blaze smoldering in Clayton's eyes that was incinerating her. Her breasts felt heavy and ripe, begging for his touch, and her stomach quivered as she undid the button on her slacks. She was the one to initiate this scene. She was reaching out and offering Clayton not only her body but her trust. Some deep-seated intuition inside her knew she could trust Clayton. Clayton would keep her safe.

She read the hunger burning in his gaze and felt a feminine power, knowing she was the cause. She also felt vulnerable and open. To offer oneself so freely was dangerous. "I'm seducing you, Clayton."

His "Oh" came out in a strangled gasp.

Her fingers trembled so badly, it took her three tries before she could lower the zipper. *Was that all he had to say, "oh"?* "Is it working?"

He cleared his throat. "Definitely." He shifted his weight in the chair and tugged at his inseam. "Perhaps, too well."

A satisfied smile curved her mouth as she pushed the slacks over her hips and down her legs. She easily stepped out of them and kicked them away to join the growing pile of clothes. She hadn't planned on going this far alone. She had been hoping Clayton would take some initiative and help her. "Are you planning on staying in that chair all night?"

"I'm afraid if I stand up, you'll disappear into thin air and I'll awake with nothing to show for this dream but rock-hard frustration."

She placed her hands on her hips and sighed. Here she was standing five feet away in nothing but a lacy bra and matching panties, and he thought he was dreaming. "I assure you, Clayton, I'm the real thing." She took a step closer to his chair and ran her fingers across her abdomen to the fancy stitched elastic on her panties. "Touch me," she whispered. "Let me show you I'm not a dream."

His gaze never left the golden skin of her slightly curved abdomen. Slowly he reached out and stroked the silky skin. In wonder he whispered, "You're so warm."

Alice leaned her head back and closed her eyes. His fingers stroked and caressed their way over her midriff. Heat poured from his fingertips, igniting small fires wherever he touched. "Do I feel like a dream?"

"You feel like heaven."

She let out a small gasp as his hands spanned her waist and pulled her closer. Her outer thighs brushed against the heavy cotton of his pants as he hauled her to stand between his legs. His fingers dug into her hips as he groaned and placed a kisses over her naval. She shivered with excitement as his tongue dipped into the hollow.

He lifted his gaze to hers. Fire met fire. "Are you sure?"

She threaded her fingers into his hair and pressed his mouth once again to her stomach. Her answer was a simple yes.

Clayton circled the enticing naval twice before dipping his tongue back into its crevice. He raised his head and eyed the creamy breasts overflowing the lacy cups of her bra. His fingers reached up and unclasped the front closure. Pale twin mounds filled his palms. He tested their weight and marveled at how perfectly they filled his hands. His thumbs brushed over the dusky, rigid nipples. He smiled as a moan of pleasure tore through her body.

"Even in my dreams you weren't this beautiful." He brushed a moist kiss across each nipple before giving the soft mounds a final squeeze. "Kiss me, Alice. Show me this isn't another dream."

Who could possibly refuse such a simple request? Alice lowered her head and captured his lips in a kiss that was guaranteed not only to prove he was awake but to show him exactly what he had been doing to her. Her tongue swept into his mouth and mated with his. Sparks erupted, heat flared, and the flames of passion ignited into an inferno. She pressed her body more fully against his. The soft cotton of his shirt teased her hard nipples into tighter peaks.

Clayton leaned back into the chair, pulling her with him. His hands caressed her back, her hips, her thighs. The scant lace covering her bottom did little to discourage his exploration of her body. His fingers slipped under the elastic and cupped her rounded derriere. He dragged his mouth away from hers and trailed a string of kisses over her jaw. "Alice?"

She moved deeper into his embrace and rocked against his body. "Clayton?" She nipped at his ear. She could feel the rigid strength of his arousal pressing against the front of her panties. Heat scorched the golden curls beneath the lacy barrier while hot fingers kneaded her bottom. Liquid passion was dampening the lace with every gentle squeeze.

He groaned and tried to hold her hips still as she unbuttoned his shirt. "We should go upstairs."

Alice impatiently brushed aside his shirt and stroked the fine curls covering his chest. Who wanted to stop and walk up a flight of stairs? Her fingers wove their way through the thick curls and flicked over his nipples.

"What's wrong with firelight?" Her mouth greedily followed the same path.

Clayton stroked the inside of her thighs and teased the moist lace between her legs. "I love firelight." He shivered as her fingers found the buckle on his belt. When he felt his zipper lower, he stopped breathing. She delicately stroked the length of him through his underwear. He grabbed her wrist. "We have to slow down, Alice." Lifting her hand, he tenderly kissed the palm. "I want our first time together to be perfect."

She flexed her hips forward. Need was spiraling out of control. She needed Clayton, and she needed him now. "Please, Clayton," she begged.

His fingers glided up her thigh and beneath her panties. Moisture coated his finger as he found her tight opening and slid inside her heat. "Lord, you're so wet for me."

She parted her thighs and tried to receive more of him. Her hips jerked against his hand. She needed more. Her hands fumbled with his pants as her mouth sought his.

Clayton felt her need. Its slick moisture welcomed his fingers. Its cry was in her harsh breathing. His control snapped. This was the woman he loved, and she was pleading with him to take her, to satisfy the ache inside them both. There would be plenty of time later for soft beds and whispered words. Now there was only this burning need.

He raised her hips and with one hurried sweep removed her panties. While still holding her, he raised himself and pushed down his pants. He retrieved a red foil packet from a pocket before kicking the trousers off his legs and out of his way.

Alice's knees bracketed his thighs as he prepared himself. She nipped at his lower lip and whispered, "Thank you."

He took her mouth in a long, slow kiss that promised heaven. Then his lips skimmed her throat and the curve of her shoulder. He lifted her and teased her taut nipples with his lips and tongue. With great care he positioned her over his straining shaft and slowly lowered her, stretching her dewy walls to fit his size.

Her thighs trembled and her breath rushed out as he filled the aching void. She felt complete. She felt whole.

Clayton swallowed hard and forced his hips not to move. Alice needed time to adjust. The tight walls cradling his manhood was testimony that it had been a long time since she had been with a man. Still, his hips instinctively thrust upward in a primitive show of possession. She was his!

Alice's eyes widened at the strange sensation Clayton's movement caused. She met his next thrust as the sensation coiled tighter. Her hands clutched at his shoulders while his mouth pulled the sensitive buds of her breasts. With his next thrust she knew she had never visited this magical place he was taking her. She quickened the rhythm, eager to see where they were heading. Eager to explore.

She heard his groan and felt his fingers dig into her hips. She rode harder, matching him all the way. The ride turned frenzied and she was no longer in control. The coil tightened, ready to snap. She gripped Clayton harder and held on as her world shattered around her. His name tore from her throat as she spun out of control. "Clayton!"

His arms convulsed around her as he shouted her name and thrust one last time, the spasm of release shaking his body.

EIGHT

Clayton ran his fingers through Alice's long hair and carefully unsnarled some of the tangles. Making love in a chair had some definite advantages, he mused. He wrapped an arm tighter around the woman cradled on his lap and felt her warmth press closer. He waited until his breathing had slowed nearly to normal before asking, "Comfortable?"

She placed a kiss over his heart. "Does the word *pretzel* mean anything to you?"

Making love in a chair also had some disadvantages. Crippling your partner could well be considered one. "Do you have any feeling in your legs at all?"

"Not for the last ten minutes." She wiggled her hips and chuckled when he groaned. "The numbness only goes as high as my thighs. The rest of me seems to be working perfectly."

He cupped her chin and forced her to meet his gaze. "Cut that out." If she continued to squirm around, he wouldn't be held accountable for his actions.

She pouted prettily. "Why?"

"You may have picked this first place to make love, but you won't pick the second." He had never had a woman react so honestly to his lovemaking. Alice was open and free with her every response. She gave as good as she got. There were no hesitancies, no falseness, no timidness. She knew exactly what she wanted, and as luck would have it, she wanted him.

"I didn't pick this ridiculous place." She brushed back his shirt and stroked his collarbone with the tip of her tongue. "You did."

"Stop that." He tried to push her away, but ended up pulling her closer. It was embarrassing to realize he was sitting there with his shirt and socks still on. "How can you say you didn't pick this chair when I distinctly remember you saying you preferred the firelight to a nice soft bed?"

"It was your fantasy to make love by firelight." She brushed the ends of his hair with her fingertips while nipping at his earlobe.

"What's your fantasy?" His hands stroked the slick, moist skin over her hip. He was full and hard again inside her. He could detect the subtle changes of her body as she responded. Her breathing was quickening, her nipples were hard nubs brushing against his chest, and the moist walls of her womanhood contracted around him. She wanted him again.

"I know one thing my fantasy isn't," she said.

"What's that?"

"To make love again while sitting in this chair." She

glanced down at their connected bodies. "I wasn't joking about losing the feeling in my legs, Clayton."

He stood up with her in his arms. "Why didn't you say something sooner?"

She chuckled and wrapped her arms around his neck. "The timing would have been terrible, trust me." She gasped suddenly.

"What's wrong?"

"I do believe they're waking up now."

Clayton reached for the afghan that was spread across the back of the couch and dropped it to the floor in front of the fire. After lowering Alice onto it, he briskly rubbed her legs. He died a thousand deaths as she moaned and tried to jerk her legs out of his grasp. "Easy, love, it will be better in a moment."

She closed her eyes and lay still. "It's getting better." She sighed as his hands caressed and kneaded their way from the tips of her toes to mid-thigh.

Clayton was having a hard time concentrating on the task of restoring circulation to her legs. The curves of her calves teased the palm of his hands with their perfection. The soft, sensitive skin behind her knees felt like satin. And creamy-smooth thighs went clear up to a thatch of golden curls guarding heaven's gate. In the cramped chair he hadn't had the opportunity to explore the wonders spread out before him. The amber glow of the fire illuminated the dewy softness of her skin. He picked up her foot and placed a kiss on the instep. "How are they now?"

Her voice came out in a rusty squeak as his lips brushed her ankle. "Better."

He unbuttoned his cuffs and removed his wrinkled shirt, then his socks. "It's getting awfully warm in here, isn't it?" His fingers trailed up her calf and over her knee as he lay down beside her. He couldn't get enough of her. He could spend the rest of the night gazing at her beauty.

"Must be the fire," she whispered. She ran her hands over his shoulders as if molding their size and shape to memory.

Check that last thought, Clayton told himself. There was no way he could spend the night gazing at her when her hot little hands were flickering over his body like wildfire. He leaned over and captured her mouth in a kiss that matched the wildfire. With a heavy groan he stroked the silky underside of her breast, glorying in the feel of her rigid nipple thrusting against his chest.

Her fingers stroked his back, dipping into the curves and smoothing over the bulges. A moan of passionate need vibrated in her throat as her hands slid lower and clutched his firm buttocks.

Clayton felt his hips involuntarily jerk forward. His rough thighs pressed into her smooth ones. His arousal brushed the curls between her legs. "Do you know what happens when you play with fire?"

Surprisingly strong fingers gripped his hips. "You get burned," she replied in a hushed voice. She raised her legs and wrapped them around the back of his thighs. She was open and ready for his loving. Her mouth swept over his jaw, looking for its mate. "Make me burn, Clayton," she pleaded.

With one smooth thrust he plunged into her heat

and allowed the flames to consume them both once again.

Alice slapped a granola bar into Clayton's out-stretched hand and ignored his laughter. It was his fault that she hadn't had time to cook a decent breakfast and that they were going to be late for work. She had wanted separate showers while he'd opted for conservation and togetherness. Saving the environment had won. Making love in a chair was child's play compared with slippery porcelain and a slick bar of soap. A tide of red flooded her face as she remembered every wanton and wonderful thing she had done last night and this morning with Clayton. The man was truly inspirational.

He studied the lone bar resting in the palm of his hand. "This is it?"

She slammed another foil-wrapped bar on top of the one he already had. "It's either this or the drive-through at the golden arches." She slid her feet into her navy pumps and slipped on her suit jacket.

He brushed the tight knot of hair at the back of her neck with his fingers. "I like your hair down better." His lips skimmed the tempting flesh her hairdo left exposed. "But this style does have its advantages."

A shiver of desire drifted up her spine. The man was dangerous. "Stop that."

"I'm hearing an 'or else' in there," he mumbled against her neck.

She tilted her head forward and gave him a better access. Desire flared to life. With a simple touch he could make her want him with an unending passion. "Or else we are going to be *very* late for work."

His lips nuzzled her throat as his hands pulled her farther back against his body. "We could call in sick?"

Alice reluctantly stepped away from him, took a deep calming breath, and picked up her purse. "Speaking of calling in sick, two of my assistants are out with the flu."

Clayton chuckled and wiggled his eyebrows as he straightened the collar on her blouse. "There seems to be a lot of that going around now." He helped her on with her coat and reached for his own. "High temperatures, body aches . . ."

Alice's laughter joined his as she opened the door. She was suffering from all those symptoms and a few he hadn't mentioned, but she didn't think a doctor could prescribe something to ease her distress. Unless the doctor happened to be Clayton.

Alice quietly closed her office door and sighed in relief. Finally, a half hour of peace and quiet with no interruptions. Beverly, a full-time student and a part-time employee of the library, was more than qualified to handle anything that came up in the next thirty minutes. She opened the blinds that had been obscuring a view of a small patch of trees and a distant farm that bordered the northern boundary of the campus. A frown pulled at her mouth as she turned her desk chair around and faced the dismal view. The fields were dry and brown and the trees had lost most of their colorful leaves. Dreary gray clouds blocked the sun and a fierce wind was scattering the dried leaves and an occasional scrap of paper. Fall was just about over, and winter was nipping at the countryside.

She raised her coffee mug and took a sip of the hot drink. A box of coconut cream patties lay open on her lap. She needed the energy and a place to think, somewhere Clayton wasn't. She reached for the first patty. What the hell had happened last night?

Looking at the scene that had played out in the family room from a fresh perspective, she realized that couldn't have been her. Or could it? She glanced down at her sensible navy suit, one of six that she owned, and the high-necked white blouse with its silver throat pin, and groaned. When had she turned into such a prude? She never used to be.

She silently chuckled as she finished the coffee and reached for another patty. Last night she had been anything but a prude. A fiery flush swept up her cheeks. Clayton must think she was either the easiest female he had ever made love to or the most desperate. She was neither. The reason she had reacted to his touch had come to her that morning while she was helping one of the students unravel the mysteries of the microfiche machine. She was falling in love with Clayton.

The one thing she'd promised herself she would never, ever do again she was doing. She was falling for another dreamer. Alice's fingers trembled as she reached for another patty. She could forgive herself for falling in love with James. She hadn't known he was a dreamer until the opportunity arose for him to choose a different dream from her own. Looking back on it now, she admired James for having the courage to follow his dream instead of settling for hers.

Loving Clayton was another matter. The man had dreams other men couldn't even begin to fathom. His dreams could put to shame all of the Jorgensen brothers' dreams together. If the rumors flying all over the campus were true, he and the five other scientists holed up in the super-equipped lab in what used to be the old administrative building were working on time travel. His sudden appearance in Maude's parlor Halloween night confirmed some type of travel. But what kind? Clayton was very closemouthed about the project he was working on. In fact he never mentioned it. Wasn't it a little strange that a man who spent the kind of hours he did in the lab did not speak of his work at all? Was it because he was sick of it and needed some relaxation time, or was he forbidden? From what she'd heard, a person needed a security clearance even to enter the building. Clayton was dreaming dreams he couldn't even talk about.

She picked up another chocolate-covered patty. She should have had more for breakfast than an oatmeal-raisin granola bar. With a groan she popped the calorie-laden patty into her mouth. She had more important things to worry about right now than four hundred extra calories finding their way to her hips. She had to figure out a way to stop falling in love.

Still staring out the window, she watched as the clouds darkened. The weatherman had obviously been wrong with the morning's forecast of partial sunshine and highs in the lower 40s. It looked like they could get their first snow of the season that night. It would be a perfect night to snuggle up in front of a roaring fire with Clayton. She muttered a curse as her cheeks heated once again and she plucked up another candy. Half the box was gone and not one brilliant idea on how to stop falling in love had entered her mind.

She closed the lid on the box, sealing off the remaining tempting candies from view. Maybe there wasn't anything she could do about Clayton. What was done was done. But now that she knew she was falling in love with him, she should be able to stop the plunge. She had to put the whole affair into its proper perspective. He was a healthy male with a healthy sexual appetite, and she was a healthy female who turned to mush every time he looked at her. Great. That was one hell of a perspective.

Alice stood up, dropped the box of candy into her bottom drawer, and closed the blinds. On second thought she reopened them. The dreary day matched her mood. She was heading straight for a heartache, and there wasn't much she could do about it. Love seemed to be as unpredictable as the weather.

Two hours later Clayton quietly opened Alice's office door and smiled. She was busily typing away on her computer and muttering under her breath. Lord, how he'd missed her, and it had only been four hours since he'd kissed her good-bye in the parking lot. He stepped into the book-lined office and shut the door. "Have you ever been ravaged in this office?"

She jumped and spun around. "Clayton!"

He placed the bags he was carrying on the corner of her desk and hauled her up into his arms. "Who else were you expecting?"

She brushed his lips with hers. "Well, Kevin Costner does stop by occasionally about this time."

Clayton reached back and locked the door. "That should take care of him." He captured her smiling mouth in a heated kiss. His arms tightened around her as he leaned against the door and savored the feel of her responsive body pressing up against his. The instantaneous fire that always burned between them ignited. He groaned as desire boiled through his blood and flowed to his groin. Within two minutes of entering her office, he was hard and ready. Alice was going to be the death of him. He couldn't think, he couldn't work. Hell, it took all his concentration just to breathe whenever she was near him. He broke the kiss and gulped in huge amounts of much-needed air.

"Does this mean I'm about to be ravaged?" she asked hopefully.

He gently moved her away from him before he took her up on her provocative suggestion. "No, it means you're about to be served lunch."

"Lunch?"

"Yes, lunch." He handed her a bag from the campus cafeteria.

"But I already have lunch." She pointed to a container of yogurt, still untouched, sitting next to the keyboard.

Clayton shook his head at the sight of the yogurt and started to clear a space on her desk. He marveled at how neat and organized she was. Four bins were stacked on one corner, each marked with its contents. A small selection of books were neatly arranged between matching bookends. The calendar blotter was spotless, and even the stapler was in line with a silver pen set.

He shuddered at what her reaction to his desk would be. The team had one security-clearance secretary between them. They had all agreed to use the secretary's amazing skill of typing over ninety words a minute to enter data onto the computer instead of having her perform any mundane tasks such as making coffee, running for lunches, or trying to keep everyone organized. Clayton's desk was his own domain.

A computer took up most of it, along with empty coffee cups, stacks of papers, and chains of paper clips. His colleagues had lost patience with him when a stack of papers slid off his desk for the third time in one day. Thinking they would shame him into establishing some type of filing system, they had jokingly emptied a cardboard bucket that chicken had been delivered in, wiped it out, and filled it with his papers. Much to their dismay he liked the bucket with red chickens printed on it and kept it. After weeks of working with it, he could locate anything he needed faster than any other member of the team. He thought, however, that Alice wouldn't appreciate his method of organization.

He glanced again at the lone cup of yogurt. "That's not lunch, Alice." He pulled out a large paper bowl filled with a chef salad and a small container of dressing and placed them directly in front of her chair. "This is lunch."

She grinned. "How did you know I like salads?" She sat down as he pulled out a cheeseburger and french fries for himself. Two cans of soda completed the meal.

"I've been living with you for over a week now." He pulled up the extra chair in the office and made himself at home. He liked the sound of that, living with Alice. Someone to come home to every night. Someone who would care if he even came home instead of spending another night at the lab. He wanted to be part of a family again. His heart lurched with need.

"You watch what I eat?" she asked.

He grinned rakishly. "I've been watching everything you do." He dipped a french fry into a blob of ketchup. "I've never seen you drink milk without adding chocolate first. You use a teaspoon of sugar and cream in your coffee, and you like your toast burned black and smothered in strawberry preserves."

She jabbed a hunk of lettuce and a strip of ham. "You could have found all that out by sharing one breakfast with me."

"Let me see what else I've noticed." He noticed the way she avoided making eye contact with him and grinned. She was putting on a pretty good front, but it annoyed her to know he had been observing her. "You like soft, lacy underthings next to your skin no matter how you try to hide the fact that you're a woman beneath those ugly suits. You have a cute little scar from when you had your appendix out when you were nine." He leaned in closer and held her startled glance. "And you make the most provocative moans in the back of your throat when you come."

Alice's fork fell into the bowl.

He picked it up and placed it back in her trembling fingers. "I didn't find out those things from eating breakfast with you."

She dropped her gaze to her salad. "Did you bring me lunch just to embarrass me?"

"Embarrass you? Embarrassing you is the last thing I want to do." He watched the emotions play across her face. Out of all the ones he'd expected her to show, embarrassment wasn't one of them. How could she possibly be embarrassed by what they had shared? It had been the most profound experience of his life. "Are you embarrassed by what happened last night?"

Her gaze shifted from the salad to a spot somewhere over his shoulder. "I guess *embarrassed* is the wrong word."

"What is the right word, Alice?"

"Confused."

His eyebrows drew together in a scowl. "About what?"

"You, me. Us!" Her arms waved in the air as if searching for the right words, ready to pluck them directly from space. "Clayton, nothing like that has ever happened to me before." Her hands fluttered down to the top of the desk. "The woman who was with you last night wasn't me."

A rakish grin spread across his face. For a moment there he thought she might have regretted their night together. "Answer me one question, Alice."

"What?" she asked reluctantly.

"Who was the woman who kissed me right there"—

he pointed to a spot directly in front of the door—"not five minutes ago?"

Alice stared at the closed door and chewed on her lower lip. "That was me."

"That was the same woman who made love in the firelight last night and who shared my bed all through the night and stole most of the covers. She's also the same woman who could give a new meaning to the phrase *taking a hot shower.*" It was on the tip of his tongue to tell her he loved her, but he bit back the urge. Alice seemed to be having difficulties adjusting to their lovemaking without adding the burden of emotional guilt. *Patience!* He must learn to be more patient with Alice. All of this was happening so suddenly, even he was having a hard time adjusting. He could only imagine what she must be going through.

He cupped her cheek and forced her to meet his gaze. "If it makes you feel any better, nothing like that has ever happened to me either." His thumb stroked her lips. "What happened wasn't embarrassing, Alice, it was beautiful. Breathtakingly beautiful." He saw the wonder shining in her eyes and sighed. "And you are right, it was also a little confusing."

"Meaning?"

"I've dreamed about making love to you for days, Alice." He dropped his hand from her face and captured her fingers. "Believe me when I say I'm truly sorry Maude's sister fell and broke her hip, but I could have thrown a party when Maude and Herbert said they were leaving."

Alice ducked her head and hid a smile.

"When we made love, I expected the thrills and excitement. What I wasn't counting on was the rightness of it all. There was no awkwardness, no hesitancies, no holding back."

"Are you saying I threw myself at you?"

"I think it might have been the other way around." He chuckled at the look of bewilderment clouding her face. "What I'm trying to say, which I'm doing a lousy job at, is that last night was perfect, Alice. It doesn't get any better than that. Something special happened between us." He knew his end had love supporting it, but what did she feel?

"I can't argue against that, Clayton." She glanced at their entwined fingers for a moment before raising her gaze to his. "So where do we go from here?"

"One place we don't go is backward. I can handle anything as long as I get to hold you in the night." He squeezed her hand. "We'll take it one day at a time if it makes you feel better." He had his whole life in front of him to make her fall in love. "Questions?"

"Only one." A lighthearted smile brightened her face. "Do I really steal the covers?"

He laughed. "Yes. Now, eat your lunch."

She speared a strip of cheese. "Speaking of lunch, what would you like for dinner?"

He lowered his cheeseburger. "That's what I really came here for."

"Dinner?"

"No, to tell you I won't be home until late. I didn't want you going to any trouble on my account."

She raised an eyebrow but continued to eat. "Working late?"

"Always." He looked for a sign of resentment in her expression and found nothing but understanding. "The other scientists all worked late last night."

"And you feel left out?"

"No, I'm feeling guilty as all hell." His gaze fastened on her mouth. "Well, maybe not *that* guilty." He liked the way she smiled, all soft and womanly. "My mind hasn't been on my work lately and I feel I owe it to them."

"Honestly?"

"Well, there's that and . . ."

"And you're scared to death they might make some great breakthrough and you won't be there to share the glory."

"No, I was thinking more along the lines of preventing a disaster if they happen to stumble down the wrong rabbit hole."

"Is that what happened on Halloween? Did you stumble down the wrong rabbit hole?"

"I ended up with the White Rabbit and the Queen of Hearts, didn't I?" He liked the way her mind worked. She was fast to pick up on a subject, maybe too fast. How was he ever going to keep Alice and his work separate? His colleagues had thought it strange when he started to refer to incorrect turns in the project as wrong rabbit holes. He'd never explained about Alice's or Maude's costumes, or about the crazed psychic calling the police.

"No, Clayton," she said. "You ended up with the real Alice."

He grinned and started to clean up the remains of his lunch. "That I did, sweet Alice." He tossed the bag into the wastebasket at the side of her desk. "I've got to be heading back now."

"Do you want me to hold dinner or leave you a plate in the refrigerator?"

"No, I'll grab something here." He tossed her his keys. "I want you to take the car home."

"But it's your car."

"You would have driven yours this morning if I hadn't insisted on you coming with me."

"I usually walk to and from work anyway. It's just a few blocks. I was only going to take my car because we were running so late."

"Then it won't kill me to walk home tonight." He bent down and brushed a slow, sweet kiss across her lips. "Please, I don't want to worry about you walking the streets at night, Alice."

"But it's okay for me to worry about you?" She lightly jiggled the keys.

"Alice . . ." He sighed in exasperation.

"Fine. I'll drive home and I won't save you any dinner." She dropped the keys into the pocket of her jacket.

Clayton backed toward the door. He didn't like the sudden gleam that had leaped into her eyes. "What am I missing here?"

Alice glanced back out the window. Definitely snow. And with any luck, inches of the white stuff. "I hope you have a pair of boots at the lab, Clayton."

"Boots?" He unlocked the door and opened it. The noise of the busy library filled the office.

"And some thermal undies too."

"Why would I need thermals?"

She chuckled as Beverly stuck her head in with some urgent request. "You'll see, Clayton, you'll see," Alice said before giving Beverly her undivided attention.

NINE

Alice pressed the bags between her body and the back door as she dug through her purse for the key. Clayton must have taken his copy of the house key off his ring before giving it to her in her office. She shivered as another blast of arctic air hit her, sending a fresh shower of snow against her face. She had been right. The low pressure system had dipped down farther than the weatherman had predicted, bringing with it the first snowfall of the season. Two inches were already on the ground, and it wasn't letting up. It looked more like Christmas was two weeks away rather than Thanksgiving. Just as her fingers located her keys in the bottom of her purse, the door was yanked open.

Alice, five shopping bags, and a freezing gust of air went tumbling forward. The shopping bags scattered, her purse spilled its contents all over the kitchen floor, and snowflakes danced around the room before melting. Alice landed in Clayton's arms. Her arrival had taken him by surprise, and he had to take a quick step or two to regain his balance.

"Alice!" His arms tightened around her.

"Who else were you expecting, Frosty the Snowman?" She backed out of his arms and quickly closed the door before drifts started to appear in the kitchen.

"Where were you?" He bent down to help her pick up the bags.

Alice glanced between the bags and him and sighed. She took a plastic garment bag from his hand and draped it over the back of a kitchen chair. Two new suits were nestled in that bag. One an eye-popping red with huge black buttons, and the other was made out of turquoise silk. The bags clutched in his hands contained a silk scarf to go with the turquoise suit, two pairs of high heels, an assortment of lacy undergarments, and a warm, fuzzy robe that somehow managed to be both practical and sexy. "Where do you think I was, Clayton?"

"Shopping!" He stared at the packages as if it was the first time he saw them. "You went shopping in a blizzard?"

She laughed and hung her coat on a peg by the door. "This is not a blizzard, Clayton. Where did you live before, Florida?" She knelt on the floor and started to shove everything back into her purse.

"I lived most of my adult life in Boston." He handed her a tube of lip gloss, a pack of tissues, and her glasses. "What's me living in Boston have to do with you risking your neck by going to the mall?"

"I wasn't risking my neck, and you should know this won't amount to much. It will probably all be melted by tomorrow afternoon." She reached for his outstretched hand and stood up. "It wasn't even snowing when I left the campus and headed for La Porte."

"What possessed you to go shopping in La Porte when you knew it was going to snow?" He glared as she smiled. "And you knew it when you gave me the warning about boots and thermal underwear."

"I didn't *know* know, I took a guess. I'd been watching the clouds roll in and the temperature drop all morning. I put two and two together and came up with snow."

"So why go shopping?" He ran his fingers through his hair in frustration.

"Because you were right." She reached up and quickly kissed him, then gathered up the packages and the garment bag.

"About what?"

"This suit." She glanced down at her unflattering navy suit and frowned. "It is ugly." She headed for the doorway. "Have you eaten yet?" Without waiting for his response, she continued, "I grabbed something between shops, but I'm sure there must be something around here I could heat up for you."

"I already finished off the rest of the ham Maude left in the refrigerator."

"Good." She kissed him again, just to see what a scowl would taste like. It tasted just like one of his everyday kisses, only harder. "I'm going to run upstairs and change into something a bit more comfortable and warmer. Why don't you go start a fire in the family room? It's a perfect night for snuggling." She remembered snuggling with him last night in front of the fire and wondered if they would repeat their performance.

She had come to the conclusion after lunch that there wasn't much she could do about falling in love with Clayton. She had wanted to taste life. Well, she was now sitting at the head table in the smorgasbord of life. She had a choice: Either get up and leave or taste every delectable dish set before her. She gave Clayton a meaningful smile before slipping out of the kitchen and heading for the stairs. She was going to savor every morsel. Because once Clayton left, and he would eventually leave, she would only have these memories. But, oh, what memories they would be.

Alice gave a yelp of surprise before pulling the covers back over her head. "Dammit, Clayton, where did you have your hands, in the freezer?"

He stopped disrobing and rubbed his hands briskly together before sliding them over her hips again. "Better?"

She slapped at the frozen fingers. "Cut that out." She tried to move over, but she was already clinging to the edge of the mattress. "What were you doing?" She had awakened fifteen minutes ago only to discover she was alone in Clayton's bed. She had wondered where he had disappeared to at first light, but she hadn't been curious enough to leave the warm haven. By the feel of his hands she would guess he had been either outside making a snowman or down in the kitchen cuddling a frozen roast.

"I was shoveling the driveway and walk." He slid naked in between the sheets and pulled her warm body against his.

Alice came fully awake with a scream. "Clayton!"

He nuzzled her behind her ear. "Hmmm . . ."

Warmth was returning to her shocked body. Her nipples that had beaded with the cold were staying hard pressed against his chest. "Next time you decide to shovel the walk, try putting on some clothes first."

His mouth caressed her shoulder as he chuckled and slid a leg in between hers. "But Mrs. Whitehall from across the street won't have anything to stare at then."

"It's Miss Whitehall, and she can go find her own man to ogle."

"You can't wear that to work," Clayton growled. He had just stepped into Alice's bedroom to see if she was ready to leave. He hadn't been expecting the sensational, sexy woman standing before her mirror. Turquoise silk draped her body like a lover. All the gold buttons on the jacket were fastened, but they still left an incredibly low-cut V across her chest. She had modestly tucked a brightly printed scarf around the collar and lapped it over the gentle swelling of her breasts. The scarf should have made the suit demure, but in fact it only helped to draw a man's gaze to the tempting ripe fruit below. He knew every incredible inch of her gorgeous body and he sure as hell didn't want any other man speculating on what lay beneath the silk suit. Alice was his.

She glanced back in the mirror and frowned.

"What's wrong with it?" She turned sideways and then completely around, gauging it from every view.

Clayton continued to scowl, trying to come up with a reasonable explanation as to why she shouldn't wear the fabulous suit to work. Frustrated by his own lack of creativity, he threw up his hands and barked, "Because it's not ugly."

Alice pressed her hand over her mouth, but couldn't hold back the uncharacteristic giggle that emerged. "You want me to wear ugly clothes?"

He touched the wisps of golden hair that had escaped her new hairstyle. Instead of the tight, unbecoming bun, she had swept the golden mass up and away from her face and fastened it in a loose chignon. Soft tendrils framed her face. The style was sexy, feminine, and begged for a man's fingers to thread their way into it and pluck out every pin.

"I want you to wear potato sacks, a football helmet" —his gaze slid down her body to caress her long, shapely legs perched on a pair of high heels that matched the suit —"and army boots."

She couldn't prevent the laughter that bubbled up out of her throat. "That's an inspiring image. I hope that isn't some deep-seated fantasy you just described, Clayton. Because if it is, Freud, himself, would have to rise from the grave to figure it out."

"No, that's not my fantasy." He lightly toyed with one of her gold button earrings. The back of his fingers caressed the silky skin beneath her ear. "What would you say if I suggested you change into that nice, sensible suit you wore yesterday and pull your hair back into that proper little bun thing?" He caressed her moist lip with the pad of his thumb. "After work you can change back into this outfit, darling, and I'll take you to any restaurant you want."

She grinned and shook her head. "I have a better plan, sweet cheeks." She picked up her purse and headed for the door. "I'll keep this outfit on and you can still take me to the restaurant of my choice."

"I've created a monster," Clayton groaned as she disappeared down the hall. He quickly followed and came to a screeching halt as his glance collided with the rhythmic sway of her hips. There seemed to be an awful lot of sass in her caboose this morning. He ran his finger around the edge of his collar as the heat rose, then with a vicious yank loosened his tie. He never should have let her get on top this morning. Power could be deadly in the wrong hands. His gaze followed her down the steps as a grin spread across his face. Oh, but what a way to go!

"Yes, Maude, for the fourth time everything is fine," Alice said into the phone. She gave Clayton a stern look as he ran his fingers over her ankles and under the hem of her robe. "Yes, *your boarder* is being very helpful." Maude's boarder had been very helpful a half hour earlier in the shower. Their Sunday brunch had been interrupted by Maude's phone call.

Clayton grinned, wiggled his eyebrows, and kissed the delicate instep of her foot.

Alice raised her gaze to the ceiling and gave her foot

another useless tug. "Tell George that I just sent him all his mail and that Clayton has been going through his house at least once a day just to make sure everything is fine." She shut her eyes as Clayton's lips nuzzled their way up her calf. "Of course it's not an inconvenience, Maude. Clayton seems to be enjoying himself immensely being the man around two houses."

She listened as Maude chatted on about all the sightseeing she and George had done. "That's nice, Maude. But if you and George have visited all those places, who's taking care of Martha?" Her leg jerked upward and collided with Clayton's eye as she shouted, "Herbert!" Her gaze shot to Clayton's face, and she frowned as he pressed his hand over his eye. "Herbert's taking care of Martha?" She tried to pull his hand away so she could see his eye, but his hand wasn't budging.

"That's nice, Maude," she mumbled, trying to keep up with what Maude was saying. Clayton didn't appear to be in utter pain, just shock. "Yes, I know Thanksgiving is Thursday, and no, for the third time, I'm not flying to Baltimore." She rolled her eyes. "I'm perfectly capable of roasting a turkey, Maude." She squinted at Clayton, who was gazing back at her with one eye. "No, I won't be all alone. Remember Dr. Williams, Maude? He happens to be living here, too, and from what I can gather, he'll be sticking around for turkey day." She matched Clayton's grin with one of her own.

"Of course I'm going to miss you and Herbert," she went on. "Martha needs you, Maude." She listened for a moment more before adding, "I'll call you in a couple of days. Give Herbert and Martha my love and tell George to behave himself. I love you too. Good-bye."

She gently replaced the receiver and sighed.

"So how's the family?" Clayton asked. He still had one hand over his eye.

"Herbert has the hots for Martha and is catering to her every wish. George and Maude are acting like tourists and have taken in every sight within a two-hundred-mile radius. Everybody seems to be enjoying themselves."

He grinned. "There seems to be a lot of that going around lately."

"Acting like tourists?"

"No, love, enjoying oneself."

She reached up and lowered his hand from his eye. A faint red blotch marked his cheekbone. It didn't look serious. Her fingers tenderly stroked the spot. "Does it hurt?"

He moaned. "Immensely."

She brushed the mark with her lips. "Better?"

"Some." He pulled her on top of his lap and caressed the knee that was peeking through her robe.

Her lips feathered across his nose and down his cheek, seeking his mouth. "How about now?"

His hand stroked her thigh, moving higher with every caress. "Getting there."

Alice silently questioned, *Getting where?* but continued to rain little kisses across his face until she encountered his hungry mouth. Her lips nuzzled and her teeth softly nipped at his lips. She wrapped her arms around his neck, and a groan of desire escaped her as his hand caressed her hip beneath the robe. She broke the kiss and in a ragged voice whispered, "How's your eye now?"

Clayton parted her robe and feasted his gaze on her beauty. "It's a miracle, Alice." He cupped her breast and flicked a thumb over the protruding nub. "Your kisses have cured me."

Her hands brushed aside the lapels of his robe and stroked his chest. "If you think my kisses have cured you, wait till you see what the rest of me can do."

Clayton swallowed hard as she pulled on the sash on his robe. "Be careful with me," he pleaded.

She chuckled as her mouth followed the same path her hands had just taken. Being careful with Clayton was the last thing she wanted to do.

An hour later Alice snuggled deeper into Clayton's embrace and planted light kisses across his chest. "Clayton?"

"Hmmm?" He tightened his hold on the warm, cuddly woman lying across his body.

"I know I already told Maude you were staying for Thanksgiving, but are you?"

"Why wouldn't I?"

She raised her head. "Don't you want to spend the holiday with your family?"

Strained minutes ticked by before Clayton slowly answered. "I don't have a family, Alice." Her research into his life obviously hadn't been that thorough.

"What about your parents?"

"My parents were both killed in a car accident when I was sixteen."

She hugged him closer and whispered, "I'm so sorry."

He felt a wet tear roll down his chest. Alice was crying! He cupped her chin and forced her to look at him. "Hey, no tears. It happened a long time ago." He gently wiped another tear clinging to her lashes. No one but his grandmother had ever cried for him before. He hesitated a moment and studied the questions gleaming in Alice's tear-filled eyes. A sad smile tugged at his mouth. "My parents were wonderful people, Alice. They wouldn't have wanted you to cry over them."

"Do you miss them?"

"Always. I miss having a family around."

"What were they like?"

"Normal, average parents. Dad was a lineman for the phone company, a nice, secure job. He went to trade school, and his greatest goal in life was to one day make supervisor. Mom worked in a department store in the housewares section. She spent her days color-coordinating tea towels, wiping fingerprints off the stainless-steel pots and pans, and dreaming about all the babies she and Dad were going to have. When I came along, they were informed that my mother couldn't have any more children."

"No brothers and sisters?"

"Afraid not." He tried to smile but failed. "Mom and Dad were born to be parents. They should have had a house full of normal kids instead of me." He pulled Alice closer and rested his chin on the top of her head as he stared up at the ceiling. "I remember the day the results from my I.Q. tests came back and I was hailed a genius. Mom just smiled and hugged me, saying that instead of having four average children she was blessed with one child with four times the average amount of intelligence."

"Was it hard on them when you went away?"

"If it was, they never showed it. Mom and Dad had known I was different since I was about six months old. They always supported me and tried to give me as much of a normal family life as possible. Weeks after I was enrolled in the special school, Dad took a transfer and they moved within twenty minutes of the school. I was allowed to go home every weekend. Most of the time I arrived home with at least one friend in tow. They even used to visit me about once a month after I started at M.I.T. It was a long trip from South Carolina, but they were always there."

"Your parents must have been very special."

A rough patch of tears clogged his throat. "Yes, they were."

"It must have been hard on you when they died."

"My mom's mom, Grandma Farry, was there to help hold all the pieces together after they were gone."

"I would have liked to have met them."

"They would have loved meeting you." Clayton gently grabbed her shoulders and held her away. His gaze bore into hers as if he wanted to read the secrets of her soul. "What would you do, Alice, if you had a genius for a son?" It was one of his biggest fears concerning a family. What if his children inherited his intelligence and his wife couldn't or wouldn't accept them? Many of his friends in the special school had parents who never visited them, parents who were happy to get rid of their "strange" child.

Her response was swift and sure. "I would love him."

Clayton's smile lit up the room. He read the truth in her eyes. With a rough jerk he hauled her back up against him and showed her exactly how a genius made love.

Clayton pushed away the empty plate where his second slice of pumpkin pie had been not two minutes before. Thanksgiving was quickly turning into his favorite holiday. It wasn't because of the succulent, moist turkey, mounds of stuffing, sweet potatoes, cranberry sauce, or the pumpkin pie he had just consumed. It was because of the gorgeous woman sitting across from him, Alice.

Even her name sounded like home, family, and happily-ever-after. Alice had gotten into Thanksgiving more than she had Halloween. She had food-shopped Tuesday night while he worked late. She had baked three kinds of pies Wednesday night while he worked late again. All the late hours had paid off, though, and the team had declared a five-day holiday. He wasn't due back in the lab until Tuesday morning. Of course the chicken bucket stuffed with papers, a briefcase that was bulging at the seams, and a borrowed computer were now taking up the entire dining-room table. Alice had good-naturedly accepted the fact they would be eating Thanksgiving dinner in the kitchen.

He had a gut feeling Alice could accept a lot, maybe even his ungodly hours. She was the essence of goodness. She was the essence of his own existence. He wasn't falling in love with her any longer, he *was* in love with her. Unequivocally, indubitably, absolutely, without a doubt in love with Alice. For weeks he had been sharing her body and bed without uttering those three little words that would tell her how he felt: *I love you.* He was terrified of saying that to her. Not only because it would be the first time in his life he had said it but because he wasn't sure how she would react.

Weren't women supposed to be clingy, immediately planning weddings and picking out china patterns at the first sign of love? Alice wasn't any of those things. In fact she seemed to go out of her way to be the opposite. None of her clothes managed to find their way into his closet. Her personal items were all kept in her bathroom down the hall. She never mentioned a future, with or without him. It was as if she was living for today, and only today. He didn't understand it, and he sure as hell didn't like it, but he knew enough not to push her into something she might not be ready for. In the past weeks she'd been like a beautiful butterfly emerging from a cocoon. Her clothes had gradually changed from dull and puritanical to attractive and bright. He both applauded and frowned at the change.

Being in love had brought out some overly protective instincts he hadn't known he possessed. He wanted his butterfly all to himself. He was stumped as to how to achieve that particular goal.

He glanced at Alice over the rim of his coffee cup.

She was breathtakingly beautiful with her cheeks all rosy from the warm kitchen and her lips still red and swollen from his kisses. He smiled at the memory of how they had spent their evening waiting for dinner to settle before digging into dessert.

He had poured out his heart about missing his parents and about their untimely deaths. He had even discussed his grandmother's death a short two years after his parents'. Her response had confirmed everything he believed about her. She was loving, caring, and definitely should have a family of her own.

"Can I ask you something personal?" he said to her now. During the past weeks he had found out a lot about Alice, but she still seemed to be holding back a lot of information, and even after all his talk about his parents, she never once mentioned her own.

"Sure." She raised a brow and lifted her coffee cup.

"You're intelligent, gorgeous, caring, and incredibly sexy."

"Thank you." A blush stole into her cheeks. "So what's your question?"

"Why aren't you married?"

Her cup landed in the saucer with a rattling clunk. Coffee sloshed over the sides, spilling onto the fancy white tablecloth she had pulled out for this festive occasion. "Why do you want to know?"

Clayton reached for her trembling hand. "You don't have to tell me, love, if you don't want. After living with you for weeks, I can't figure out why somebody hasn't come along and snatched you up."

"You make it sound like I'm some fish swimming in a lake with a flock of starving eagles circling above."

"Eagles don't travel in flocks, so let's not change the subject." He held her gaze. "You possess only one fault that eliminates you from being perfect."

"And that is?" Her shoulders drew back and her chin rose a notch.

"You steal the covers every night." He grinned at her offended look. "Don't worry, love, I'll keep you. Perfect people bore me." His fingers entwined with hers. "So tell me why you aren't married. I find it hard to believe no one has ever asked you."

Alice released his hand and dropped a couple of turkey-printed napkins onto the spill. "I was asked once." She continued to study the splash as if it held the past. "I even accepted. His name was James David Keating. I met him my junior year at college and we were to be married the summer after we graduated. I already had a job promised to me at the library, and he was going to be an elementary school teacher. We picked out a small little Cape Cod on the other side of town where we could have some privacy but where I wouldn't be too far from Maude and Herbert. We were going to wait five years and then start our family, two children, one boy and one girl." She picked up the soaked napkins and place two dry ones on the spot.

Clayton waited what seemed like a very long time before reluctantly asking, "What happened?"

"The week of our graduation James was offered a chance to go to some remote village in Honduras and work with underprivileged children. The Peace Corps already had a doctor and an agricultural specialist, but they needed a teacher, one who was fluent in Spanish and loved working with children."

"He left you to go work in Honduras?"

"No, Clayton. He left me to fulfill a dream." She raised her gaze to his. "James always had a burning desire to help children, especially the poor. Here was his chance to help an entire village."

He studied the calm look in her eyes. Alice wasn't still in love with this James character. She was too serene for her heart to be bleeding. "Why didn't you wait for him, or go with him? Don't Peace Corps volunteers have only two-year stints?"

"The week he told me, he started to talk about the next village, and then the next. That's when I realized it wasn't a one-shot dream, it was his lifelong dream. I'm not the type of person who could live in some primitive village in a foreign country for the rest of my life. I have responsibilities here."

"What happened?"

"I loved him enough to let him go."

"No regrets?"

"No. I realize now it would never have worked out."

"Ever hear from him?"

"About two years ago I got a letter from him. He's still teaching in remote villages. He married the doctor who went down with him and they now have a son. They're planning on single-handedly pulling Honduras into the modern world."

"That must have hurt." Maybe he had been wrong in

assuming she wasn't still in love with James. Maybe she was still suffering from what that jerk did to her.

"No, Clayton." She smiled at his concern. "I stopped loving James years before the letter came. I still have fond feelings for him, but not love. I sent their son a set of miniature trucks and I also enclosed a bank draft to help purchase medicine and books for the village."

"That was nice of you."

"No, what was nice was receiving back a huge stack of handmade thank-you cards from the children." She stood up and cleared the table of the cups and plates.

"I'm going to go out on a limb here and make a guess." Clayton carried over the silverware and loaded it into the dishwasher. "I bet you've made more than one donation to the Honduras fund, haven't you?"

She picked up the tablecloth, placed it in the sink, and filled the sink with water. "Every six months James, Barbara, and little Dylan make it out of the jungle and into town. I make sure something is waiting for them there."

Clayton came up behind her and wrapped his arms around her waist. He gently brushed aside her hair and nuzzled her neck. So much for her past, now onto her future. "So you want to have two children and a Cape Cod."

She chuckled and leaned back into his embrace. "No. I wanted six children, but I compromised down to at least two, and I wanted a huge old monster of a house, but James wanted something new and maintenance-free."

His arms fell to his sides and his lips froze against her neck. In a strangled voice he asked, "Six kids?"

"Yes." Ignoring his startled response, Alice added a drop of detergent to the coffee stain and rubbed it briskly. "So, Clayton, why aren't you married?"

"Me?"

She liked reversing the tables on him. He was adorable when he was off balance. Since he was the one who was always asking questions, maybe it was time for some questions of her own. "Yes, you. From what I've seen, you seem like a pretty good catch."

"Are we back to the fish-in-the-lake theory?"

She grinned and brushed her lips over his chin before turning back to the tablecloth. The stain seemed to be gone. "You have a few bad qualities, but nothing that should keep you off the market."

"What bad qualities?"

"You're a slob, for one."

"I'm not a slob!"

"Okay, maybe *slob* is too harsh of a word." She tapped her finger against her chin. "I've got it, you're disorganized."

He glared down his nose at her but couldn't argue with the truth. "What else?"

"You can't cook."

"I thought that was a quality that husbands look for in a wife."

"Get real, Clayton. These are the nineties. Wake up and smell the roses."

"Didn't I help you cook today?"

Alice laughed as she drained the sink and wrung out

the tablecloth. "Washing the turkey, lifting the roasting pan into the oven, and opening a can of cranberry sauce isn't considered cooking, Clayton." She opened the laundry-room door and tossed the tablecloth into the washer to be washed first thing in the morning.

"What about my work?"

She shot a quick glance at him before turning away. "Having a good job is considered a plus in the marriage market."

"What happens if the job is a tad consuming?"

"Meaning?" She avoided his probing glance and concentrated on rearranging the napkin holder and the colorful bouquet of chrysanthemums Clayton had brought her yesterday.

"You know, long, hard hours, some weekends, bringing the office home with you."

Clayton nervously toyed with the damp washcloth as he watched her face. What was she hiding? His work was his life, at least it used to be until she waltzed in and stole his heart. Now his work rated a distant second. He'd never had to worry about what someone else thought about his long hours or lost weekends in the lab. He needed to know if his career was going to be a wedge between them. So far, she'd been awfully nice and understanding whenever he missed dinner or worked late.

"Hard work never hurt anybody," she said, glancing around the kitchen as if to make sure everything was neat and tidy. She turned on the dishwasher and asked, "Do you want to go take a stroll through George's house to make sure everything is all right before I call Maude?"

She was hiding something. He could feel it, but he

didn't know what. Whatever it was, it concerned his job. If she wasn't resentful of his long hours, what else could it be? Was she upset because he didn't talk about it? Most of what he did in the lab was boring and repetitious. It was also classified. He wondered how the other members of the team handled their spouses. Did they say it was classified and never discuss it? Or did they talk about some of the problems and their achievements? It had never bothered him before that he couldn't talk about a lot of his work. But now it did. He wanted Alice to be a part of his life, a major part. She should have the right to know what was going on when he left her bed every morning. Secrets, even classified ones, shouldn't exist between a man and his wife.

Clayton wearily ran his fingers through his hair. What if they had children? His own son or daughter wouldn't even know what he did. Little Clayton junior couldn't go to show-and-tell and tell the rest of the kindergarten class what his daddy did. Other dads would be firemen, lawyers, doctors, mechanics, and little Clayton junior would just have to shrug his shoulders and say he didn't know.

He helped Alice on with her coat, then grabbed his off the peg. Oh, Lord, this being-in-love bit was a lot harder than he had expected.

TEN

Alice closed her office door and leaned against it. Peace and quiet surrounded her like a lover's embrace. Clayton's embrace? She smiled and moved away from the door. Clayton's embrace was never peaceful or quiet. With the slightest touch he could inspire raging passion and soaring desires. Anything but peace and tranquillity to both her body and mind.

Over the past few days her quiet, peaceful library had turned into the main gathering place for almost every student on the campus. Final exams were coming up, and the rush was on to suck in every particle of information. Students every semester mistakenly sought a quiet corner between the towering shelves to cram for an upcoming exam, hoping the knowledge contained in all the books that surrounded them would mysteriously seep into their pores. It never worked. A person would have to study on the fifty-yard line at a Notre Dame football game to get more privacy. Well, maybe not that bad, but some days it seemed like it. She rubbed her aching temples. Today was one of those days.

She could handle the chaos and the endless questions from the students. It was her job. That was what the university was paying her for. It was handling Clayton she had her doubts about. She had promised herself she wouldn't fall in love with him. Even when she'd realized she was, she had convinced herself she could handle it. But it was all a lie. She couldn't handle it. Every day, instead of being more aloof and in control, she was just the opposite. Clayton had not only taken total control of her body, he had squeezed into her heart, maneuvering his way into every nook and cranny. The damn thing couldn't even beat any longer without calling his name, Clay-ton, Clay-ton, Clay-ton. She was doomed to a life of loneliness.

That piece of disturbing knowledge had come last night, around four A.M. She had awakened from a sound sleep to discover Clayton was gone. His pillow still showed the indentation from where his head had rested, but the sheets were cool. She had glanced around the room and at the empty bathroom before pulling on her robe and heading downstairs. She had found him where she'd known she would. He had been sitting at the dining-room table merrily tapping away at the keyboard and conversing with the main computer back at the lab. He had pulled on a pair of jeans and an old sweatshirt. Thick socks warmed his feet and a new pair of glasses, because he never had found his old ones, were perched on his nose. His hair had been rumpled and tousled from where she had run her fingers through it during their previous lovemaking.

She had leaned against the doorway and studied him. The two empty coffee cups beside the keyboard testified to the length of time he'd been at it. Clayton always forgot to carry the empty cup when he went back for a refill, so he usually ended up with an array of cups scattered about when he worked. The five-day break he'd had at Thanksgiving had shown him it was possible to work at home, linked to the main computer back at the lab. He had explained to her that the other scientists already worked that way at times. He, on the other hand, had always claimed he needed to be right there in the lab to concentrate and achieve anything worthwhile. Thanksgiving break had shown him otherwise. Alice wasn't sure if she was happy about this discovery or not.

After watching him work for fifteen minutes without being detected, she had sighed and headed back for the warm comfort of his bed. He might be able to survive with three or four hours of sleep a night, but she needed at least seven in order to be able to hold any kind of intelligent conversation before noon.

After she had crawled back in between the covers, it hit her how lonely it was without him. Was this how it was going to feel after he left? She had spent the remainder of the night staring at the ceiling hugging his pillow and fighting back tears.

Alice glanced around her office and frowned at the stack of mail piled high in the incoming tray. She hadn't had a chance to look at the mail in two days, something totally out of character for her. Maybe she should take a page from Clayton's book and take her work home with her? No, that wasn't fair. Clayton never worked at the computer unless she was asleep. Occasionally when they snuggled up on the couch together in the evening and she wanted to watch something on television that didn't interest him, he picked up one of his many articles, journals, books, or magazines, and they'd spend the evening curled up in each other's arms doing two totally different things. They went to bed by eleven, and every night Clayton woke around three or four and sneaked downstairs to his second office.

Clayton had been right about one thing. He did misplace things. *Lose* was too strong a word, because everything eventually turned up, usually found by Alice. She had finally set a box on one of the dining-room chairs so that she had a place to stack everything that had found its way throughout the house. Newspapers with articles circled, letters, faxes, and journals popped up in some amazing places—bathrooms, on top of the washing machine, the backseat of her car, on tables in the upstairs hallway. Anyplace was susceptible to being used by Clayton.

His laundry landed in the hamper, on the bathroom floor, in the bedroom. His saving grace was he never expected her to do it. Shoes were scattered around the house, and it had came to the point more than once that Clayton had to decide what to wear by the pair of shoes he could find. Alice was amazed at how well he kept track of his leather jacket, until the day she realized he owned three identical ones. His only explanation was that he really liked the jacket and saw nothing wrong with owning three. That fascinating twist of logic had made her fall even more in love with him.

Alice sat behind her desk and picked up an envelope and her letter opener. Clayton was due to pick her up in about twenty minutes to drive her home, and, barring any emergencies, she just might get through all of her mail. He'd insisted that he drive her back and forth to work since the night of the first snowfall, refusing to listen to her about walking instead. Most evenings after dinner they would walk around the entire block just to check out George's house.

How was she going to manage without him? Now that she'd tasted life, she wanted more. She needed more. She needed to dream again. But Clayton was the wrong man to dream about. He wouldn't be staying in Harper. He was a man who would follow his dream, wherever it led him. Even if she didn't have Maude and Herbert to worry about, she couldn't go galloping into the sunset with Clayton and his wild dreams of the future. She had some dreams of her own, which included an old monstrous house and six children. With a heavy sigh she slit open the first envelope.

Clayton glanced up from the computer screen. His gaze encountered the sleepy stare of the woman he loved as she leaned against the archway into the dining room. "What are you doing up so early, sleepyhead?" he asked.

Alice smothered a yawn with the back of her hand. "I couldn't sleep."

He quickly saved the file he was working on before

standing up and walking toward her. "Miss me?" he asked hopefully.

"Yeah." She reached up and ruffled his already messed-up hair. "I didn't have anyone to fight over the blankets with."

He chuckled and kissed the end of her nose. Lord, she looked good enough to eat. All warm and soft from his bed. He felt the hot flash of desire surge into his groin. "No fun to steal them off yourself, is it?"

"Nope." She glanced at the table. Three empty cups sat near the keyboard. "How long have you been up?"

He backed her against the wall and flexed his hips against hers. A rakish grin spread across his face. "I've just started, love. Give me a chance."

She chuckled and splayed her fingers over his chest. "Are you ready to come back to bed?" She nuzzled his throat. "I promise not to steal any more covers off you tonight."

Clayton growled deep in his throat, cupped her pert little bottom, and pressed himself harder against her. Would he ever get enough of this woman? He feared the answer was no. He would go to his grave still wanting her. The woman he loved, Alice. He wanted not only her body but her warmth. He needed everything she had to give. She surrounded him with love and something else he desperately needed, a sense of family. Without her he wouldn't be whole. He slowly shook his head and held her gaze. "How can you make me want you so?"

"Me?" she squeaked. "It's you that does this, not me." She brushed back a lock of his hair that had fallen across his forehead. "I just came downstairs to see what you were doing."

"Jealous?" He shouldn't have asked the question, but he had to know. Alice was extremely tolerant about the time he gave to his work, but he was half hoping she had come downstairs to lure him away from the computer.

"Jealous of your work?" She glanced at the blue computer screen and shook her head. "No, Clayton. I know how important your work is to you."

He noticed a sadness lurking beneath her quiet statement. "Do you think it's more important than you are?"

"It's who you are, Clayton."

"No." He placed a finger under her chin and forced her to meet his gaze. "It's what I do, not who I am." He brushed a kiss across her mouth. "Don't you know how I feel about you?"

Her hands slipped under his sweatshirt and flattened against his back. His muscles tensed beneath her stroking fingertips. "I guess you like me."

"Like you!" he exclaimed, astounded. She thought he only liked her? He cupped her face, then lowered his hands down her neck and over her shoulders. The lapels of her robe gaped, giving him an enticing glimpse of the sweet, pale curves of her breasts. "I do much more than like you, Alice. Much more." His thumbs tenderly stroked her satiny skin, dipping lower with each caress.

Alice held her breath as his fingers inched their way closer to her breasts. "That's nice."

"Nice?" He shook his head as the robe gaped farther and her breasts with their pert nipples filled his hands. He slowly bent and lavished each nub with a wet kiss.

Raising his head, he trailed his tongue over her trembling lower lip. "It's not nice, Alice. It's called love."

Huge blue eyes filled with wonder, hope, desire, and confusion stared back at him. "Love?"

The pad of his thumb followed the same path his tongue had just taken. "Why so shocked?" He'd thought she knew. He thought everybody knew. Sometimes he was surprised to look in the mirror in the morning and see that the words weren't written across his forehead in neon letters. His co-workers surely knew it, and they'd teased him unmercifully until they realized that by being in love, he was coming up with some brilliant ideas on how to spend more time at home instead of in the lab. As far as the team was concerned, they all hoped that the woman who'd hooked him was reeling him in and would be frying him up at the altar of holy matrimony real soon.

"I . . ." Alice swallowed hard twice and continued to stare at him. "I . . ."

He grinned. "Are you speechless?" He never thought to see this day.

"No, of course not," she snapped. In a softer voice she said, "I just wasn't expecting you to make any declarations, that's all."

A frown wiped away his self-assured grin in a flash. "Why not?"

"Well . . ." She glanced around the room as if looking for help. "With your job and all . . ."

"My job!" He thrust his fingers into his hair and scowled at her. "What in the hell does my job have to do with me loving you?"

"I . . ." Her glance shot toward the computer as a beep penetrated the room.

Clayton glared at the offending machine but quickly returned his attention to her. His voice returned to a normal level. "Alice?" He had obviously caught her by surprise, that was all, he told himself.

"Yes?"

He bent down and kissed her, then raised his gaze to hers. "I never said these words to another woman, so I'm probably doing it all wrong, but I love you." Tears, of what he prayed were happiness, filled her eyes.

Her smile was watery as she encircled his neck with her arms and pressed herself against him. "Do you know what is so special about those words, Clayton?"

He started to maneuver her toward the dining-room table that was behind him. The sash of her robe had come undone, and her naked body pressing against him was more than he could stand. "What?" He shoved a stack of papers off the table and onto the floor.

"I happen to be in love with you too."

He jerked his gaze back to her face as another beep pierced the room. Lifting one hand, he touched her face —the sweet arch of her cheekbone, the sweep of her nose, the tilt of her chin. Blue eyes moist with emotion stared back at him. Love was burning in their depths brighter than any fire he had ever seen. "Do you have any idea how badly I need you right now?"

For her answer, she pulled his sweatshirt over his head and tossed his glasses in the general direction of the keyboard. Another beep came from his computer. She smiled as he laid her on the dining-room table. "I think it's jealous of us."

"Computers don't have emotions," he answered absently. His jeans hit the floor with a soft thud, and he stood before her hard and erect. She looked beautiful lying on a wave of white chenille with her golden hair capturing the glow from the overhead chandelier. His fingers trailed up her pale, smooth legs. "Tell me again," he begged.

She twisted her fingers into his hair and pulled his mouth down to hers. "I, Alice Elizabeth Jorgensen, love you, Clayton Williams, with all my heart." She took his hand and placed it over her wildly beating heart. "With all my soul, and with all my body." Her mouth sealed her declaration with a kiss to end all kisses.

Clayton thought he would die from heart failure before he could prepare himself to enter her. In one swift plunge he joined their bodies. Her heat surrounded him, pulled him deeper within her, and eliminated any rational thoughts but one. He loved her and she loved him. The pace he set matched the wild pounding of his heart.

Alice wrapped her legs around the back of his thighs and matched him thrust for thrust. In the heated strains of their lovemaking the computer continued to beep and the table groaned with their combined weight. She moaned his name and whispered words of love.

Clayton felt the tiny convulsions that shook her body as she found her release. Her satisfaction sent him over the edge, and with one last mighty thrust he arched his back and joined her for the ride of his life.

The weight of Clayton's body felt like heaven. Warm, hairy-chested heaven. Alice's breath was slow in returning to normal as she squinted at the dazzling chandelier above them. Her fingers wove through the moist hair sprinkled across his chest. She turned her head and glared at the computer as another beep pierced their haven. "I don't think your computer likes me."

Clayton chuckled against the soft pillow of her breasts and opened his eyes. Glancing at the screen, he groaned. Aaron Cheever was demanding to know where he was. Clayton had been on line with the main computer and Aaron when Alice had entered the dining room. Aaron, like himself, found it easiest to work in the early-morning hours before his family awoke.

"Don't worry, love," he said to Alice. "It's not you the computer's calling names, it's me."

"Why?"

He took most of his weight off her and pulled the keyboard closer. "It's only Aaron wondering what happened to me." He started to type an answer.

"Do you mean to tell me you were talking to a real person on that thing?" She grabbed the ends of her robe and covered herself.

Clayton chuckled at her attempt at modesty after what they had just done. "Don't worry, Alice. He couldn't hear or see us." He threw his leg over her so that she wouldn't get up as he finished typing his message to Aaron. "It's not like a phone."

"I know that!" She glared at the man and the machine. "It's just embarrassing, that's all."

"He doesn't know what we were doing." He brushed

a kiss across her cheek as he signed off. "In fact he doesn't even know you were in the room."

Alice continued to glare at the screen. "Well, I'm just relieved that I'll never have to face Aaron. I would probably die of embarrassment."

Clayton glanced down at her red swollen lips and grinned. "That reminds me. There's something I forgot to tell you."

"What's that?"

"We're invited to a Christmas party in two weeks."

"Where?"

Clayton glanced at the computer and then sheepishly back at her. "Aaron's house." Before she could do more than groan her despair, he brought his mouth down on hers and made her forget all about Aaron, computers, and Christmas parties.

Alice glanced in the full-length mirror and slowly turned around. She had a hard time believing the woman staring back was she. The once-prudish and prim image was really shot to hell now. Two days ago Clayton had announced that he was taking her somewhere special that night. Someplace where they could dine and dance the night away. She had spent the entire afternoon at the mall finding just the right dress. A dress that would make Clayton forget all about dining and dancing and make him concentrate on the more important things in life, such as making love to her. She had been torn between two dresses and ended up buying both. Aaron's Christmas party was less than a week away and she would need something special to boost her confidence when she faced the man. No matter how much Clayton reassured her, she still believed Aaron had to have known something was happening.

She turned back around and glanced over her shoulder at the back, or rather the lack of back, of the dress. Wherever he was taking her, she prayed the heat would be turned up high. But then again, with Clayton she probably would be warm enough even in an igloo. She had taken the time to sweep up her hair into a sophisticated style and use a faint amount of makeup. If Clayton said it was going to be a special evening, she wanted to hold up her end.

She picked up her new clutch purse and dropped in a few essentials—lipstick, tissues, a couple of dollars, a credit card, and as Maude always instructed her, a quarter just in case she needed to make a phone call. She smiled as she snapped the purse closed.

For the past week she had been walking around with her head stuck in the clouds. Or was it buried in the sand like some ostrich? She didn't for one minute disbelieve that Clayton loved her. She felt his love in his touch, in the way he kissed her, and in the tremor in his voice each and every time he told her. And he told her often. Not just when they were making love but during a good movie or even a rotten movie, while sorting out their dirty laundry together, and he even called her at work to tell her. She hadn't thought it possible, but she grew to love him more with each passing day.

He had embedded himself so deeply into her heart, it was going to take a cardiac surgeon to remove him once he left. She knew this couldn't continue forever and that one day Clayton would tell her that his work in Harper was done. But like the ostrich, she simply buried her head deeper in the sand. She would deal with his leaving when it happened. For now she wanted to live and love.

She picked up the black sequined jacket that went with the dress and put it on. The cool silk lining caressed her back and arms. She straightened the gold cross necklace that had been her mother's. It was one of the precious few possessions she had of her parents'. Fred and Gayle Jorgensen hadn't been known for their material possessions. They had been too busy chasing their dreams to gather a bunch of belongings. They had been too busy chasing their dreams to give their only child the security and stability she desperately needed. Their dreams had ended with their deaths, and so had one of hers. She would never feel again the sweet hug of her mother or the strong arms of her father as he tossed her up into the air and caught her.

Alice blinked her eyes and willed the tears away. No more tears. No more broken dreams. She didn't dream about a future with Clayton, so there was nothing to be shattered. Just because they proclaimed their love didn't change anything. They'd been lovers before that announcement, and they were lovers still.

She studied her face in the mirror one last time to make sure the near tears hadn't smudged the light coating of mascara she had applied. After a couple of deep breaths she turned off the light and headed downstairs to join Clayton.

His room was empty as she walked past. She frowned

momentarily when she thought about tonight. Why was he taking her someplace special? She didn't believe the excuse he'd used that morning about wanting to dance the night away with her in his arms. There had been a peculiar gleam in his eyes when he said it had nothing to do with dancing.

Hours later Alice found herself wrapped in Clayton's arms on a postage-size dance floor. The floor was deserted except for two other couples. Most of the diners had left hours ago. She nuzzled the soft lapel of his suit with her cheek. "You weren't kidding when you said you wanted to dance the night away."

"Tired?" He gave her a gentle squeeze, then ran his hand down her back again.

"Of dancing with you?" She glanced up and smiled. "Never."

He pressed her face against his chest again and continued their slow movement around the dance floor. "I think our piano player is about to call it a night."

"I know. Even Cinderella had to leave the ball sometime."

He chuckled. "Have I told you how incredibly beautiful you look tonight?"

"Three times, but who's counting." Her arm wrapped around his waist and she hooked a finger into the back waistband of his slacks. "Did I thank you for the lovely bouquet of roses?" When she had arrived downstairs, he had been waiting for her in the formal parlor with a dozen long-stemmed red roses.

"Three times, but who's counting." His feet came to a stop as the music softly died. "We could turn on the stereo at home. I'm sure Herbert has something appropriate for dancing in his collection." He escorted her back to their table and helped her on with the sequined jacket. "You aren't planning on wearing this dress to Aaron's Christmas party, are you?"

"Why, what's wrong with it?" She picked up her purse and headed for the cloakroom. "Don't you like it?"

"There's nothing wrong with it, Alice. That's the problem. How am I supposed to enjoy the party if I'm too busy slugging my colleagues for drooling all over you?" Clayton handed the girl behind the counter their claim tickets.

"You say the sweetest things, darling." She batted her eyelashes and winked at the girl as she was handed her coat. Clayton helped her put it on. She noticed the generous tip Clayton gave the girl and suppressed a smile.

"Come on, brat," Clayton teased as he ushered her outside. "If you behave yourself on the way home, I'll let you have some champagne when we get there."

"What champagne?" she asked as she got into the car.

"The champagne that's been chilling in our refrigerator the whole time we've been dancing." He closed her door and hurried around to the driver's side.

Alice's gaze followed him around the hood of the car. She continued to stare at him as he started the car. The man was whistling under his breath! She was freezing her tootsies off and he was whistling. "Clayton?"

"Yes."

"Are we celebrating something special?"

He reached over and squeezed her knee before placing the car into gear and heading out of the parking lot. His cryptic response of "Could be" filled her with uneasiness.

Clayton pulled Alice closer and slowed his steps to barely a sway. Everything was going as he'd planned. The fire was blazing, casting a romantic glow over the room. Slow, seductive music floated from the stereo like a lover's caress, and Alice had enjoyed the first glass of champagne with him. If everything went as planned, they would be finishing off the bottle in his bed.

His only concern was her sudden stiffness. She seemed a little on edge since they'd left the restaurant. He stroked the silky skin of her back. "Is everything okay, love?"

"Fine," she said hoarsely. She cleared her throat and tried again. "Everything is wonderful, Clayton." Apparently she saw the doubt on his face and quickly added, "This is the most romantic night of my life. Dinner, dancing, roses, and now champagne and firelight. What more could a woman ask for?"

He continued to study her face in the amber glow of the flames. It was probably the bad lighting that made him read the anxiety in her eyes. "I know one more thing that would make this night more romantic." His fingers slipped down her back and lightly rested on her hips. He never should have danced so close to her. Just being in the same room with her caused his body to react; having her rub against him caused an enormous reaction, all in one aching area. An area that hopefully would be seeing some relief after he asked one very important question.

Her gaze glided down his body to the bulge straining against the front of his trousers. One golden eyebrow shot up. "And what might that be?" she teased.

He chuckled. "Not that." He laughed harder at her look of disbelief. "Well, okay, maybe later *that*." He pulled her closer to the fireplace. He wanted to see her expression. He wanted to memorize each feature of her face, every curve, so that when he was eighty, he would be able to recall this moment as if it had been yesterday.

He reached up and with the backs of his fingers touched her cheek. His voice was steady and sure as he asked the most important question a man could ask a woman. "Alice Elizabeth Jorgensen, will you marry me?"

ELEVEN

"What did you say?" Alice croaked as she took a step back.

Clayton forced his smile to stay in place. "I asked you to marry me."

"Why?" She took another step back and clutched the back of the wing chair. Why hadn't she seen this coming? She had known something was up, but a marriage proposal had never crossed her mind. This was what the dinner, dancing, and champagne had been leading up to. Heartbreak.

"Because I love you," he said, "and you love me." He took a deep breath and slowly lowered his hands that had been holding her a moment ago. "That's what people do when they're in love. They get married and start a family. You know, six kids, big old monstrous mortgage payments to match the house, night feedings, diapers, and orthodontist bills." He slid his hands into his trouser pockets, looking like a man who'd lost the script he was supposed to be following. "Alice, will you marry me and become my family?"

"I can't." She blanched as he stiffened. "I mean, I won't." Her heart screamed in agony as his shoulders started to droop. She didn't want to hurt him, but the truth now was better than heartbreak later. "I will not marry you, Clayton."

"Why the hell not?" he demanded.

She looked away from the pain in his eyes. Her fingers turned white as they tightened their grip on the back of the chair. She wanted to reach out to him. To comfort him. To hold him. She had promised herself this wasn't going to hurt. So why did it feel like she was dying inside? Clayton deserved to know the truth. She loved him enough to give him that. "I can't marry you because you're a dreamer."

"A dreamer?" He rubbed the back of his neck. "You mean like James?"

"James had dreams, but they weren't anything like yours. Your dreams are far more dangerous."

"What in the hell kind of dreams are you talking about?"

She studied the flames leaping around a log in the fireplace. Why was he arguing with her? Why couldn't he have just left things as they were? They could have been lovers for weeks longer. "What do you think our married life would be like?"

"I pictured something along the lines of that big old house with six kids running in and out of every room. I saw Maude and Herbert dropping in for visits and spoiling the kids." His voice wavered slightly. "I saw us growing old together, rocking our grandchildren, and loving."

Alice swiped at the tears rolling down her cheeks. He had pictured her dream. "Do you know what I see?"

"What?"

"I see me standing around the dinner table with our children trying to figure out a way to tell them Daddy isn't coming home ever again because he's living in a cave with the Neanderthals or fighting in the Crusades." She swiped at more tears. "I see me trying to explain why their daddy chose to step into some time-travel machine and allow every molecule in his body to be broken down and transported through space and time.

"I see me trying to hold all the pieces together while you follow your dream, Clayton." She grabbed a tissue from the box on the end table and fiercely blew her nose. "All my life I've been left standing alone while others chased dreams. First by my parents and then by my fiancé."

Clayton opened his mouth to protest.

She shook her head and stared at him till he closed his mouth. He not only looked pale, he looked as shaken as she felt. "I love you more than life itself, Clayton. That's why I can't marry you. I would never survive knowing I wasn't enough to hold you."

"Not enough?"

"Drop it, Clayton." She took a few steps toward the door. "It's been"—she worried her lower lip for a moment—"nice, but under the circumstances I would understand if you moved out in the morning."

"Move out!"

"Clayton, please." She held up a hand to stop him from advancing any farther. She had to get away before she made a fool out of herself and broke down totally. The dream he had painted was too tempting. "No more tonight. We'll finish discussing anything you like in the morning, but no more tonight." She headed for the hall.

"Alice?"

She stopped at the door but didn't turn around to face him. "Yes?"

"We haven't even begun to discuss our future."

Her shoulders stiffened and she clasped her trembling fingers together in front of her. "We don't have a future, Clayton."

"Then how come I keep seeing you with gray hair, wrinkles, and rocking our grandchild to sleep?"

Alice shook her head and ran blindly from the room. She didn't stop until she was behind her bedroom door.

With a heavy sigh Clayton lowered himself into a chair and stared at the fire. What had happened to all his finely executed plans? He knew there were some humdingers as to why women didn't marry men, but this one had to take first prize. The woman he loved, and who loved him back, wouldn't marry him because she was scared to death he would pop into a time-travel machine and disappear out of her life! Lord, by not talking about his job he had really made a mess of things.

An hour later Clayton got to his feet. He checked the dying embers and replaced the screen in front of the fireplace. His fingers automatically turned off the stereo that had stopped playing a while ago. He wasn't sure what he was going to say to Alice in the morning, but he knew he wasn't leaving.

He turned off the hall lights and made sure all the doors were locked before climbing the stairs. The key to Alice's fears was his work. He entered his bedroom and stared at the lonely, cold bed. Well, there was one thing Alice didn't know. Something that had hit him while sitting in front of the dying fire. He'd collect garbage or pump gas before he let her go. It might be a little hard supporting a wife, six kids, and an old, monstrous house on that kind of salary, but he'd do it somehow. When it came to a choice between her and his career, she would win every time. Maybe it was time that he sat her down and gave her a clearer picture of what he did for a living. The unknown had a terrifying way of coloring things.

Alice cautiously entered the kitchen the next morning. She was waiting for Clayton to pop out from wherever he was hiding. When she'd walked by his room that morning, she'd noticed that he hadn't packed. The dining room was still cluttered with his stuff, and his car was in the driveway. She didn't want to see him and she especially didn't want him to see her. She was a mess, with eyes red and puffy from a night of crying. She'd forced herself out of her bathrobe and into an old pair of jeans and the baggiest sweatshirt she could find. Her brow was wrinkled from a pounding headache, and even her hair was hanging limp in its ponytail. Horses that were on their way to glue factories had shinier-looking tails. She was about as sexy as a garden slug.

All night long she had heard Clayton's voice asking over and over again, *Alice, will you marry me and become my family?* It ripped another piece of her heart to shreds every time she heard his plea. Clayton had no one but his work. His parents and grandmother were gone. He had been on his own for sixteen years. At least she had had Maude and Herbert to cling to. Whom did Clayton cling to?

With automatic movements she plugged in the coffeemaker and put on a pot. Eating actual food sounded as appealing as eating dirt. Coffee was all her stomach could handle this morning. She had a feeling Clayton wasn't going to leave their conversation where it had ended last night. He was going to demand answers. Answers she wasn't going to be capable of supplying without at least three cups of pure caffeine.

She reached for a mug, poured the black brew, and was taking her first sip when Clayton walked through the back door. The hot liquid went down the wrong pipe, causing her to gag and cough.

Clayton saw the look of panic that swept across her red face and hurried to her side. With more force than finesse he started to pound on her back.

Alice backed away and raised her arms in front of her. Between coughs she managed to croak out, "Stop." After a few more breaths she regained control and said, "I'm fine now." She eyed his hands and frowned. He obviously didn't know his own strength. "Thank you." She flexed her shoulders and felt a soreness where he had pounded. Great, she thought. Not only was he breaking her heart on the inside, he was now trying to smash it from the outside.

"Are you all right?" he asked.

"You startled me when you opened the door, and my coffee went down the wrong way, that's all."

"I'm sorry. I didn't mean to startle you. I was over at George's checking things out." He handed her back her mug, which she had placed on the counter. "Take another sip, slowly." When she did and everything went down smoothly, he reached for a mug and poured himself a cup. Without taking off his jacket he leaned his hip against the counter and studied her.

Alice kept her gaze lowered and stared into her cup as if it was the most fascinating thing she had ever seen. She could feel his gaze upon her and was waiting for the first question. It had been awfully nice of him to at least try to help her a moment ago.

"Are you done with your coffee?" he asked.

She glanced between the empty cup and him. She gave a startled little gasp as he took the cup from her fingers and set it on the counter next to his empty one.

He clicked off the coffeemaker and handed her one of her jackets that was hanging by the door. "Let's go."

"Go where?" She shoved her arms into the jacket and automatically started to button it.

"You'll see when we get there." He opened the door and hustled her outside.

"I don't think this is such a good idea, Clayton." She came to a halt when she realized she was now locked out of her home. Clayton hadn't given her time to pick up her purse.

"You owe me this, Alice." He opened the passenger door of his car and waited.

"What's *this*?"

"You'll see."

He didn't look mad or upset, just determined. She guessed she did owe him "this," and maybe a lot more. She had known from the beginning that it was never going to work out between them. Maybe she was the one who had led him on the whole time. She slowly got into the car.

Within three minutes she knew they were heading for the university. Her confusion started when he parked in the south parking lot instead of the usual one closer to the library. Without saying a word he got out of the car and she followed. The campus grounds looked deserted for a Sunday morning. Understanding dawned as she walked beside him toward the old administrative building. They were going to the lab!

Clayton walked up to the newly installed security doors and pushed a series of numbers into a discreetly hidden box to the right of the doors. With a distinctive click the door opened.

Alice gasped as Clayton held the door open and waved her in. "I can't go in there," she said.

He glanced inside and frowned. "Why not?"

"I don't have a security clearance."

"Yes, you do." He opened the door wider and patiently waited.

"Since when?" She tried to peer into the building without looking too conspicuous.

"As of seven o'clock this morning you have the university's approval to receive a guided tour through the lab."

"How did that happen?" She edged closer to the door.

"I demanded it."

She glanced up at him in surprise. Mister Whiz Kid from M.I.T., the celebrated physicist, the man with so many initials after his name, it took two lines to address his letters, had requested that she be allowed in for a guided tour? She didn't know what surprised her more, that he'd asked or that the clearance had been granted. She glanced once more between Clayton and the darkness beyond. There was no way she was going to pass up this opportunity to see the inside of the most-talked-about building on campus. Taking a deep breath, she entered the building.

Clayton allowed the door to close behind them as he reached for the light switch. Overhead lighting flooded the spacious outer room.

Alice looked around, disappointed. She had no idea what she had been expecting, probably something out of a Frankenstein movie, but this wasn't it. Half the room was a standard waiting area, with the other half appearing to be a section for a secretary. The furnishings were all glass and chrome, and the walls and carpeting were various shades of blue. It looked neat and ordinary.

"This is Jenny, our secretary's, domain. She prefers the relative calm of this room to that of the inner room."

He waved a hand in the direction of a light-blue couch in the reception area. "I've spent more than a few hours on that, and believe me it's not as comfortable as it looks."

Alice frowned at the couch while Clayton continued to act like a tour guide. He pointed to two doors near Jenny's area. "That's the office supply closet, coatroom, et cetera, and the other door is to Jenny and Sharon's, the only women on the team's, bathroom." He headed for a set of double doors, opened one, and proceeded to flip on a row of light switches.

Alice gasped as she stepped into the room. The entire first floor had been gutted, except for Jenny's office, and converted into one huge room. She knew there were six scientists working here, so it came as no surprise to see the six separate areas on the one side of the room. She knew immediately which desk was Clayton's by the chicken bucket sitting on top. That and at least a dozen coffee cups. A huge conference table loaded with papers, computer printouts, coffee cups, a few empty pizza boxes, and a Nerf football sat in the middle of the room. The other third of the room was the computer. Hell, by the mere size of it, it could have been five computers, for all she knew. Blackboards with what appeared to her to be gibberish lined the walls, and an occasional poster was tacked up for color. There was one of Einstein near the doors, over the far desk was a poster of a Ferrari, and Clayton had a huge print of Garfield eating lasagna hanging above his desk. A vase of wilted flowers sat on what had to be Sharon's desk.

Clayton followed her gaze as it shot around the

room. "Sorry about the mess, but we don't have a cleaning staff. When it gets too deep in here, or when Sharon threatens to leave because of the stench, we all pitch in and clean it up."

Alice moved deeper into the room. "Am I allowed to walk around?"

"Sure, just don't erase anything on the boards." He pulled out one of the conference-table chairs and sat down, propping his feet up on the table as Alice wandered around the room. "You're also free to ask any question you want."

She shot him a surprised look. "Is that part of the security clearance?"

"No, that's my decision." He entwined his fingers behind his neck and relaxed. "I can't convince you how unfounded your fears are if I withhold information from you, can I?" He closed his eyes and sighed. "There will be no secrets between us, Alice, ever."

Alice bit her lip and studied Clayton. He looked ready to fall asleep. She glanced around the room. They obviously weren't expecting any company or guests this weekend, or they would have made some attempt to straighten up the place. Whatever she wanted to know was sitting right out in front of her, all she had to do was look.

She slowly walked from desk to desk. She studied blackboards and computer printouts. She even went as far as opening one of the files on Clayton's desk because she recognized the initials on the label, NASA. The folder contained fifty or so photos of outer space, computer enhancements of different galaxies, and what appeared to be black holes. She tossed the folder back onto his desk. Great, now instead of picturing herself explaining to the kids about Dad traveling the ocean blue with Christopher Columbus, she could be explaining how he was on Mars teaching little green men how to play poker.

She slowly made her way back to Clayton and stood silently by his side.

He opened his eyes. "Well?"

She shrugged, then waved her arms to encompass the entire room. "I don't understand any of it." Well, she did understand the three tic-tac-toe games on one of the blackboards, but that didn't count.

Clayton chuckled as he got to his feet. "Don't worry. I've been confounded by your Dewey decimal system a couple of times in my life." His hand reached up as if to caress her cheek, but he pulled it back before it touched her. "No other questions?"

"Thousands." She glanced down at his hand. "I just don't know where to start." Lord, how she'd missed him last night. Was that how she was to spend the rest of her life, lonely?

"Start at the beginning." He picked up the empty pizza boxes and tossed them into a trash can sitting by the doors.

"Can you travel through time?"

He laughed as he picked up an empty doughnut box and a few empty soda cans. "No."

Alice frowned. "*Are* you trying to travel through time?"

"No." He tossed the empty cans into a cardboard box marked RECYCLE. "At least not yet."

"What's that supposed to mean?"

He sighed as he carried half a dozen dirty coffee cups over to a small kitchen area in a far corner. "The ultimate goal of this team is time travel," but we will never achieve it, at least not in my lifetime."

She stared at him in astonishment. "You're working on something that can't be done?"

"No." He filled the sink with soapy water and dropped all the dirty cups in. "For the last twenty or so years the government has been keeping an eye on a bunch of people throughout the world who are experimenting with space-and-time travel. Some amazing results have occurred over the years, and even Einstein's theories of general and special relativity concur that time travel is possible. Nothing in the laws of physics prohibits time travel."

"Really?" Lord, it was all true. They were working on time travel. She nervously glanced around the room.

"Really." Clayton took apart the coffeemaker and dumped the pot into the soapy water. "The U.S. government has a couple of teams of scientists working throughout the country on various aspects. Through mutual friendships, colleagues, and universities, we formed our own team here at Harper's. The government is supporting the bulk of the project with grants, and Harper's is picking up the rest. All of us have been working on different angles of space-time travel for years. Now we use each other as partners and sounding boards.

Each of us has a specialty or a particular area in which we like to work. Together we make a well-rounded team.

"When we came here in August, we decided to concentrate on traveling through space, not time." He took her hand and led her to a set of stairs she had noticed earlier. "We call it teleportation. We figured it wasn't much good traveling just through time if you can't pinpoint where you want to land."

Alice glanced up at the top of the stairs and saw a steel door. "Can you travel through space?" That would explain Halloween.

He sighed. "Sort of. It's not anywhere near perfected. In fact it's just the opposite." He opened the steel door and flipped on another row of lights. "Our test run pointed out more faults with our venture than advantages. There are a lot of variables that we didn't allow for the first time. Such as other dimensions."

Alice stepped into the room and froze. If she thought the downstairs had gone through a transformation, it was nothing compared with this. The second and third floor of the building was now one huge room. She slowly stepped forward and stared in wonder at the machine that filled the room. Three huge laser guns were mounted about fifteen feet off the floor, and all were pointing at a shining metal platform in the center of the room. Massive machines took up the rest of the room. The whole thing looked like something out of a sci-fi movie. "Does it work?" she whispered.

"Sometimes. It's called a teleportation machine, but we named it Oscar, after the grouch on 'Sesame Street' because it's so ornery and stingy with the little it gives up." He smiled at the look of fascination glowing in Alice's eyes. "You can look all you want, but please don't touch anything."

She stepped closer. "Is this what they used on you Halloween night?"

He took his time in answering her simple question. Reluctantly he said, "Yes."

"Are you out of your mind!" she cried. "You could have been killed." She stared in horror at the towering machines.

"Or worse."

"What do you mean by *'or worse'*?"

"You know about our four dimensions, length, width, depth, and time." She nodded. "Many physicists are studying theoretical entities called strings. The term's used to describe the behavior of particles under high-energy conditions. These string theorists are convinced that there must be either ten or twenty-six dimensions instead of the four we are aware of."

"What's that got to do with the *'or worse'*?"

"We're beginning to believe they might be right."

"I don't get it."

"We did a couple of tests with Oscar here. We can send stuff, but we can't control where it lands. The scary part is, after my test run, most of what we send never reappears." He smiled slightly and shrugged. "So, where does it go?"

"Do you mean it just disappears into thin air?"

"Nothing disappears into thin air, unless another dimension exists that we aren't aware of yet. Take my glasses for instance."

"They're at home on the dining-room table."

"No. Halloween night I was wearing a pair of glasses when Oscar here shot me to your house. Thick, black glasses with my name and the university's address taped around one of the earpieces. I arrived at your house without them, nothing arrived at the landing sight, and nothing was left here on the platform. So where are the glasses?"

"They could be anywhere, Clayton. Somebody probably found them and never bothered to return them."

"True." He walked around the six-foot circumference of the platform. "Where is the crate of oranges, the coffee cups, and a dictionary that were all wrapped in paper declaring a huge reward if returned to the university? Nothing has ever turned up."

"That doesn't mean anything." She nervously moved a foot away from the platform. "Does it?"

"That's just it, Alice. We don't know, and until we do, nothing living can be teleported again. I'm sure you understand the need for security concerning this project."

She numbly nodded her head. It was all too much to digest at one time.

"Then I'm sure you will understand when I tell you we falsified our report to Congress."

"You lied to Congress!"

"Not exactly lied. More like withheld some information. If some gung-ho congressman learned of what could logically appear as a near success, Congress might want to push the project beyond the realm of safety.

Every member of this team is dedicated to taking every precaution and doing it right and doing it safely."

He led her from the room and down the stairs, holding her hand until they were across the room and he started turning off lights. He left a small light burning in the far kitchen area. "Any more questions?"

She shook her head. "I can't think right now, Clayton. It's all too much."

He stroked her cheek. "I can imagine. I'm sorry. I keep forgetting how frightening it must appear when it's dumped on you in one lump. I've been involved with this kind of work since I was twenty. I've watched and helped the field grow for fourteen years."

"You must love it."

"Yes, but not as much as I love you." He rubbed his thumb across her lower lip. "I volunteered to be the guinea pig on that test run because I was the only member of the team who didn't have a family or someone special to come home to. I won't be volunteering again, Alice. I have you, Maude, and Herbert waiting for me." His lips followed the path his thumb had just taken. "Did I mention how much some of us like Harper? It looks like at least four of us are thinking of moving here. Aaron and his wife are looking at houses this weekend."

"They are?" Alice whispered as he strung kisses over her jaw.

"Sharon is talking about starting a family."

Alice tilted her head and moaned as his mouth caressed her throat. "That's nice."

Clayton raised his head and gazed into her eyes. "Marry me, Alice?"

Cold, hard reality crashed against the sensual haze Clayton had surrounded her with. How could the man do that with just a few kisses? She had been ready to agree to anything he wanted. She shook her head and backed away. "Don't you see, Clayton, I can't be responsible."

"Responsible for what?"

"For holding you back from this dream." Her arm jerked in the direction of the room. "What happens in a year, two years, or a decade when you discover a way to travel safely through space? You'd be the first to want to go." She swiped at the tears clouding her vision as she backed out into the reception area. "What happens if you find another dimension? You'd want to go exploring."

"It's not like that, Alice."

"All this doesn't change who you are, Clayton. You're a dreamer, and I can't marry a dreamer." She turned and fled through the security door, out into the pale winter sunlight. The doors closed before Clayton's string of curses filled the lab.

TWELVE

Alice felt Clayton enter the kitchen and continued to chop carrots. For the past two days, since the morning in the lab, they had been living in the same house and acting like perfect strangers. No more than a few cordial words had been spoken. Mostly by Clayton, saying he wouldn't be home for dinner. The strain was killing Alice. Her work was suffering, her appetite was nil, and what little sleep she did get was plagued with horrible dreams she couldn't remember when she woke. The knife trembled so badly in her fingers, she had to put it down before facing Clayton. He looked as awful as she felt. "Dinner will be ready in about ten minutes."

He nodded and pulled his jacket off the peg by the back door. "I'll go check out George's house."

"You won't have to do it again after tonight."

That got his attention. "Why?"

"Maude and George are coming home tomorrow afternoon. I'm picking them up at the airport at two."

"What about Herbert?"

"He's staying with Martha. Seems the love bug bit those two. From what Maude tells me, there's going to be a January wedding."

Clayton stared at Alice as if she'd lost her mind. "Isn't love grand?" he growled, then slammed the door behind him on his way out.

Alice stared at the closed door for a long time before muttering, "No, Clayton, love stinks." She blinked back her tears and turned back to cutting up the carrots.

Clayton glared at the computer screen. Two o'clock in the morning was a hell of a time to be sitting alone in the dining room taking his frustrations out on some poor, defenseless computer. He hadn't known what to expect during the Christmas party at Aaron's that night, but he had been hoping for something, anything but the polite mask Alice had worn. He had pushed and shamed her into attending, insisting that Aaron and his wife had gone to a lot of trouble and were expecting them both. Alice had relented, put on an outfit to rival the angels, then proceeded to charm everyone at the party. Everyone, that was, except him. The polite mask slipped back into place every time he had stood beside her. If Maude wasn't upstairs sound asleep, he'd be tempted to pound on Alice's bedroom door and demand some answers. Like why in the hell was she doing this to them?

She loved him. He would stake his life on that. The last two weeks without her had been pure hell. Thanksgiving was a distant memory filled with happiness and love. Christmas was quickly approaching, and it appeared to be shrouded in shadows and sadness. Maude had been busy decorating the house for days. Garland was strung everywhere, wreaths decorated the doors, and a seven-foot Christmas tree was proudly on display in the front parlor. Christmas carols constantly filled the family room, and the aroma of freshly baked cookies saturated every room in the house. His heart gave a violent twist every time he entered the house, because as things stood, the present he was feverishly wishing for wasn't going to be sitting under the tree come Christmas morning.

Clayton glanced at his empty coffee cup and tried to decide if it was worth getting up to make another cup. Since midnight, when he'd watched Alice climb the stairs to her bedroom, he had gone through three cups and had accomplished absolutely nothing.

A slight sound from the archway drew his head around. He blinked twice to make sure his eyes weren't playing tricks on him. They weren't. Alice was leaning against the doorway. She was dressed in her old battered robe and fuzzy red slippers. The sophisticated hairstyle she had worn to the Christmas party was gone, along with the makeup and the miniature poinsettia earrings. She was plain, everyday Alice, and she'd never looked more beautiful.

"Am I disturbing you?" she asked.

"Always," he answered with a smile. He motioned to the chair next to him. For weeks he had tried to sit Alice down and show her how he could communicate with the main computer back at the lab. She hadn't entered the dining room since the night they had made love on the table. Desire shot through his body at just the memory.

Alice stepped into the room but didn't take the seat. She toyed with the back of a chair, with the evergreen centerpiece on the server, and picked at a hunk of dried wax on the side of one of the red candles. "Did I ever tell you how my parents died?"

His gaze never wavered from her face. "No, you never talked about your parents." He watched her every emotion, her every move. Something important was happening here and he didn't want to miss a minute.

"Fred Jorgensen met Gayle Harting during an expedition in the interior of New Guinea. They were both anthropologists. My mother always referred to the day she met my father as fate; my father claimed it was bad timing. Either way they fell in love, were married in an ancient ritual, and took up housekeeping in a grass hut in some isolated village."

"Sounds romantic." He wasn't sure what he was supposed to say, if anything.

Alice frowned and picked a yellowish leaf off a poinsettia plant. " 'Romantic' wasn't how either one described it. They made it back to America two weeks before I was born." She tore the leaf in half. "It seems one of the drawbacks of living in the wild is lack of birth control." The leaf was torn again. "They caved in to the pressure of their families and were married legally the same day I was christened."

"I wish your parents were still alive, Alice. They sound like very interesting people." He wished she would look at him.

"Oh, my mother and father were fascinating people, just ask anyone who knew them. They were the hit of any party, whenever they were in civilization long enough to shake the cobwebs off their fancy duds. The stories they could tell were remarkable. They seemed to have seen and done everything. Their work with little-known tribes and cultures was considered extraordinary. Universities fought to support their next expedition."

Alice took a deep breath. "Oxford University backed their last expedition into the Amazon. There were rumors of finding an Indian tribe that guarded the Lost City of Gold. My parents couldn't refuse the dual challenge of a lost primitive tribe and a legend. They didn't care about the gold; material possessions never meant anything to them." She fell silent as she stared out into the night.

"What happened?" Clayton asked when he realized she wasn't going to continue.

"No one knows. Months after they were supposed to report in, Oxford University sent in a search team. They were about three days into an uncharted section of the rain forest when they ran across what had been my parents' camp. Everyone in the camp, including my parents, had been killed."

"I'm sorry, Alice."

She tried to muster a smile, but failed. "Thanks, but it happened a long time ago."

Clayton sat back in the chair. She was still staring off into the night. "It must have been hard on you."

"What, having my parents killed when I was thirteen?"

"There's that. But I was referring to being left behind. Who took care of you while your parents were off working?"

"I was shuffled between my grandparents and Maude and Elmer while my parents followed their *dream.*"

Clayton sighed. There it was sitting directly between them, the concept of following one's dream. She had been raised by substitute parents while her real mom and dad had been busily following their own dreams that hadn't included her. Dreams that had eventually led to their deaths. Between her parents and James, it wasn't any wonder she thought that if a person had dreams, there wasn't any room left in his life for anything else, including her. Clayton wanted to take her in his arms and hold her tight. To tell her everything was going to work out, but was it? How was he ever going to get her to see his career had nothing to do with his dreams of her and of having a family of his own?

"On second thought," he said, "I don't think I would like to meet your parents. They wouldn't like what I would have to say." As for James, he was thrilled the man hadn't had the common sense to compromise, because then Alice might have married him and Clayton wouldn't have known her love.

"Don't be mad at them, Clayton. They did love me in their own way."

"A very strange way."

"Perhaps, but it must have been hard having a baby, who obviously wasn't planned, slow them down."

"I read some of the articles on your parents in the dozen or so scrapbooks that Maude's saved through the years. I didn't notice any slowdown on their part. In fact you weren't even two months old when your parents set out for a remote section of the Philippines." He stood up, saw the leery look that entered her eyes, and stretched. He purposely walked to the other end of the room. "There is something called compromise, Alice. Your parents should have seen how much you needed them and traveled only half as much, or taken you with them if it was that important to them. Lots of parents take their children with them when they travel."

"My parents trekked through uncharted regions of dense jungles. They couldn't tote a toddler around with them."

Clayton frowned. She was still defending them. "What about James?"

"What about him?"

"Didn't you tell me that Barbara and he have their son living with them? Aren't they living on some remote mountaintop in Honduras?" He took a couple of steps in her direction. "James is following his dream, Alice, with a wife and child beside him. Your parents could have, too, if they'd wanted to."

She glared at him. "Are you saying my parents didn't want me?"

He shook his head. "I never met your parents, so I wouldn't presume to know what they wanted. Only you can answer that question, Alice." He pushed a couple of buttons on the keyboard and turned off his computer. "All I'm saying is their dreams have nothing to do with you and me."

"I came down here, Clayton, thinking I could make you understand."

"Understand what?"

"Why it could never work with us. Don't you understand that I can't compete with your dreams, Clayton? I'm tired of coming in second."

"Second!" he shouted. "Is that where you think I place you, second?" He shoved a trembling hand through his hair. "When have I ever treated you like you were second?" He quickly closed the space between them and captured her chin in a surprisingly gentle hold, considering his rage. "You've been first in my heart and in my mind since the night I met you. Don't you know how much I love you?" He lowered his head and savored her sweet, trembling mouth. She tasted of minty toothpaste and tears. He swept his tongue past her lips and laid claim to all that could be. He continued to kiss her until he felt her melt against him in sweet surrender.

When he felt her tremble with desire, he pulled back and ended the kiss. "I'm going to marry you, Alice, and I'll do my best to give you those six children you've been dreaming about." He wiped away a tear glistening on her cheek. "We can work this out, love. Haven't you realized yet that we both have the same dream?" He placed a gentle kiss on her forehead before heading for the door and calling a soft, "Good night."

His step was light as he climbed the stairs and headed for a cold shower and a lonely bed. Alice had told him about her parents. It was a beginning. He now understood where her fear had initiated. With that knowledge there surely had to be a way to combat it.

Clayton came to a halt outside the kitchen archway and shamelessly eavesdropped on the conversation between Maude and Alice. A wide grin split his face as their voices reached the hallway.

"Oh, Maude, I'm so happy for you. I knew all along that you and George made a wonderful couple."

"You don't think we're too old to get married?"

"Nonsense. You're perfect for each other."

"We set the date for Valentine's Day."

"The most romantic day of the year," Alice exclaimed. Clayton could tell she was fighting tears again. At least this time they were tears of happiness.

"George wanted it sooner," Maude said. "But with Christmas and then Herbert's wedding coming up in January back in Baltimore, I told him February was the earliest we could possibly do it, so he suggested Valentine's Day."

"Impatient, isn't he?" Alice teased.

Maude was silent for a minute before saying, "There is one concern I'm having."

"What's that?"

"You."

"Me?" Alice said. "What about me?"

"I want you to know both George and I are inviting you to come live with us. George's home is roomy, and there's plenty of space for you there. We don't like the idea of you living all alone in this great big house."

"Who said I could even afford to buy this place?"

"I won't sell it to you, Alice. It's the Jorgensen's family home and you're the last Jorgensen. It's only right that you should have it."

"What about Herbert? He's a Jorgensen."

"Martha and he are quite happy to live in her house in Baltimore. Besides, Herbert and I are up in years, and there won't be any children to pass it on to, so we decided it should go to you."

"I can't accept the house," Alice said. "This place must be worth a fortune. Why don't you and Herbert sell it, split the profits, and go on honeymoons or something?"

"Sell Captain Jedidiah's house?" Maude cried.

Clayton took his cue, as if the script was written for him, and entered the kitchen. "No need to advertise, Maude. I'll take it."

"Take what?" Alice asked.

"The house of course." He walked over to the coffeepot and poured himself another cup.

"Who says it's for sale?" Alice snapped.

"Maude just mentioned something about selling, so I wanted to get my bid in first. I've been keeping my eye out for a big old, monstrous house lately."

Maude glanced between the two in confusion. "I will consider your offer, Clayton. But understand that I must let Alice decide first. After all, she's family."

Alice glared at her aunt. "You would sell him Jedidiah's house?"

"Only after you decide what you're going to do, Alice. I would prefer to keep the house in the family, but if you don't want it, we won't pressure you." She smiled at Clayton. "It would make a fine house for Clayton to set up practice in. Jedidiah would be so proud to have a doctor living here."

Clayton glanced at Alice and mouthed the words, "Practice in?" She shrugged in response.

Maude stood up and reached for her coat. "I'm going to run over to George's to tell him how happily you accepted our news. He wanted to be here when I told you, but I told him he was being old-fashioned." She tied a scarf around her head and disappeared through the back door.

Alice scowled at Clayton. "You only want this house because I do."

He dropped a quick kiss on her forehead. Two days had passed since their discussion in the dining room. She was still being stubborn and guarded. "Now you're beginning to get the picture, Alice." He started to whistle a snappy little tune as he carried his coffee to his second office. His plan to win her love and trust was almost complete. Within two days everything would be concluded and there wouldn't be anything standing in their way.

Alice slowly stood up and stretched the kinks out of her back. She had spent the entire night curled up in a chair in Clayton's bedroom waiting for his return. He never showed up. He had spent the whole night in the lab, just as he had told Maude on the phone he was going to. It had been the worst night of her life.

Every other night for the past few weeks she'd known he was right down the hall from her. Never more than a few steps away. Tonight he'd been gone, and she had never felt more alone. Was this what the rest of her life was going to be like?

She had spent the night thinking of what Clayton had told her. He was right about her parents. It wasn't their dreams that had kept them apart from her. If they had really wanted to, they could have remained a family. They hadn't wanted to. It was as simple as that. She should have seen it years ago, but she had chosen to ignore the signs. Maude and Herbert had never criticized her parents, at least not in front of her. She had a feeling they said a lot about her father and mother behind her back.

James was an entirely different story, one that she'd painted with the same brush. If she had really loved James, she would have gone with him and lived out the rest of her life in some grass hut eating insects. The truth was she hadn't loved him enough. She had been attracted to his good looks and his ordinariness. He was safe and secure, or at least he had been.

In the hours before dawn she'd come to realize exactly how much she loved Clayton. For him she would live in a grass hut, eating snakes and fighting malaria. For him she would pack up their children and follow him through time and space.

Herbert now had Martha to look after him, and vice versa. Maude had George and their newly found love to keep her happy. There wasn't anything holding her in Harper. She felt somewhat responsible still for Herbert and Maude, but nothing she couldn't handle from anywhere Clayton's job demanded he relocate to. They would be together, and that was what it all boiled down to.

Clayton deserved that family he had been dreaming about. The same family that crowded her dreams. They were both dreaming the same dream!

Alice made her way to her bedroom and a quick shower. As soon as she got to work, she was calling the lab and begging Clayton to meet her for lunch. She was going to accept his proposal of marriage, six children, and an old, monstrous house, if it was still open. And if it wasn't, she was issuing a proposal of her own he couldn't possibly refuse.

Four hours later a frazzled Alice reached for the ringing phone. The morning had gone from hopeful expectations to total bedlam. The university was gearing down for the upcoming holidays, and finals were in full swing. The library was not the place to find peace and serenity. She hadn't even had a chance to call Clayton yet; twice she had managed to dial only the first three digits of his phone number before being interrupted. The way the day was shaping up, it was going to be midnight before she'd be home to propose to the man she loved. She smiled at the thought and said, "Hello, Alice Jorgensen," into the receiver.

"Hello, Alice. This is Jenny, Clayton's secretary."

"Hi, Jenny." Alice had met the energetic Jenny the other night at Aaron's Christmas party.

"I don't know if I'm doing the right thing . . ."

There was a moment's pause before Jenny continued, "but could you come over to the lab right away?"

"What's wrong?" Alice asked, alarmed. "Is Clayton all right?"

"He's fine, Alice. But I really think you should come." She gave a startled gasp, then whispered, "I've got to go."

Alice stared at the receiver in her hand and blinked. Jenny had hung up. Something was wrong! In seconds she'd slammed down the phone, grabbed her coat, and sprinted from her office. She didn't even glance at her assistant as she called out, "Beverly, handle anything that comes up."

A dozen times in her flight across practically the entire length of the campus, she cursed high heels and their inventor. Still, she made it to the lab within minutes and jabbed at the intercom button next to the security box.

"Yes?" came Jenny's voice over the box.

"Jenny, it's me, Alice." She gasped for air and demanded, "Open up."

The doors immediately opened, and Alice hurried into the reception area. Her glance shot to Jenny, who was sitting behind her desk sadly shaking her head. "In there." She pointed to the double doors that led to the inner room. "But I think it's too late."

Alice paled but pushed open the double doors. She glanced around the room and frowned. On the hurried trip across campus she had visualized a hundred different scenarios. Clayton volunteering to retest the machine, the teleportation malfunctioning and blowing them all to kingdom come, or them accidentally pulling some-thing from another dimension into ours. Hundreds of scenarios, and nothing that even resembled reality.

She slowly walked the rest of the way into the room and looked around the conference table, where five sci-entists quietly sat. Every member of the team was there but Clayton. Surely if something dreadful had happened, they would be doing something more than sitting around looking at her. "Where's Clayton?"

"He's gone," Aaron said. He nodded toward a piece of paper lying at the head of the table.

Alice walked over to the table and started to read the neatly typed paper. It was Clayton's resignation! He was leaving the team for personal reasons and accepting a professorship in the university's science department. She reread the resignation twice while joy bubbled through her. He was willing to give up his dreams because of her.

She slowly lowered the paper and glanced at the sci-entists. No one looked pleased. "Did anyone accept this?"

"No, we all refused," Sharon said. She tapped her pen against the table. "It doesn't matter that no one accepted his resignation. We can't force him to work here, Alice."

She smiled. "Then there's nothing to prevent him from coming back, right?"

"Right," Ellis said. A lopsided smile tilted up one corner of his mouth.

Alice tore the resignation in half. Her grin grew wider and matched every member of the team's as she tore it in half again and again. "Expect him back tomorrow morning." She dumped the handful of torn paper into her coat pocket, ignored the team's cheering, and marched out of the lab.

She cussed her shoes and the frigid winter weather as she trekked her way back across campus toward the dean's office. Within minutes she was stomping the light, powdery snow, which was just starting to fall, from her shoes as she eyed the dean's warhorse of a secretary. General Grant himself would have had a hard time passing the woman.

Alice took a deep breath and smiled her most charming smile. She was a Jorgensen, and a Jorgensen always went after her dream. And her dream was in the dean's office this very minute. "Hello, may I please see the dean?"

"Do you have an appointment?"

"No, but—"

"I'm sorry, the dean is busy right now."

"I know. He's with Dr. Williams, right?"

"How did you know?"

"I need to speak to both Dr. Williams and the dean, please. It's very important."

"I'm sorry, but I can't interrupt them."

Alice lowered her gaze for a moment. So much for the polite method. "I understand." With quick purposeful strides she marched to the dean's office door and opened it.

The secretary was right on her heels as Alice stepped into the plush office. "I'm sorry, sir," the secretary said as she hurried forward, trying to grab Alice's arm.

"Alice!" Clayton exclaimed as he jumped out of his chair.

The dean stood also and surveyed the scene. "It's all right, Miss Merryweather." He smiled at Alice. "Miss Jorgensen, to what do we owe this honor?"

Alice nervously shifted her glance between the dean and Clayton as the secretary left the office, closing the door quietly behind her. "I came to tell you Dr. Williams won't be accepting the professorship you so graciously offered him." She kept her gaze fixed on Clayton. "It seems the team needs his expertise."

"I already resigned from the team, Alice."

She pulled out a handful of torn-up pieces of paper and handed them to him. "It seems your resignation got lost."

The dean hid a smile behind his hand. "I think I hear Miss Merryweather calling me." He headed for the door. "Why don't you two discuss this some more?" He let himself out of his own office.

Clayton studied the scraps in his hand. "You now have me totally confused, Alice. I resigned from the team to take a teaching job at the university so that you won't have to worry about me pulling any disappearing trips into the future. I had it all figured out. I'll teach and we'll live in an old, monstrous house and have six children."

"I'll take the old, monstrous house and the six children, but I'd have to draw the line at you teaching." She took a step closer and cupped his cheek. "It seems I fell in love with a dreamer. A man who has a vision of the future that few of us can see. A man committed to doing it right, and doing it safely. I want to marry that dreamer."

He placed his hand over hers. "What about your fear of my gallivanting through time and leaving you and the little ones behind?"

"Will you?"

"Never." He pressed her hand against his mouth and placed a moist kiss in the center of her palm. "I'll never leave you, Alice." He pulled her closer and whispered against her lips, "I love you."

"Good." She nipped at his lower lip and smiled. "But just to make sure you don't take off for a vacation through time, I plan on making every day with you so special, you won't ever dream of leaving." She reached up, and her mouth melted against his with the promise of forever.

EPILOGUE

The Eighth Dimension:

The suns were rising in the south and in the west. The time was fast approaching as the furry little creatures rolled and whirled their way across the open meadow. Waves of amethyst grass and sapphire flowers danced before the four winds. Morning was upon them, casting away the darkness and the empty hours of night.

A larger creature lovingly cradled two miniature versions of herself as she twirled her way toward the pedestal. Four long, floppy ears trailed behind her, obscuring the puffy crimson tail that marked her as a breeder, the highest status granted to a milhook without being the grand vizier. She whirled and twisted her way through the crowd until she was directly below the pedestal, at the place of honor, which befitted her stature.

Other breeders cradling their young quickly joined her. No one had missed the sunrise since the gifts from the heavens had started to appear. At first they'd been afraid and anxious as the gifts materialized out of thin air. Great confusion had prevailed through the land for many turnings of the suns. Finally the grand vizier had declared the gifts as coming from heaven, and a magnificent pedestal had been constructed in the middle of the meadow by the worker milhooks.

The next sunrise their labor had been blessed as they'd placed the first gift in the center of the pedestal. It was a strange thing made out of a dark substance surrounding a clear essence that nothing could pass through. Nothing in the milhooks' experience had prepared them for encountering a pair of glasses. Strange markings had been found on one of the narrow strips protruding from the object. The markings had been copied and religiously studied by the most learned. No one could make sense of the alien scratching, *"Dr. Clayton Williams, Harper University."*

The breeders nudged one another as the crowd grew quiet. Even the youngest milhook understood the significance of this moment. As the dual suns climbed higher in the heavens, their rays shot down on the meadow, lighting the gifts. Huge objects made out of a crinkly substance, all containing some of the strange markings as the object on the pedestal—*"Property of Harper University. Reward offered if returned. Call 555-7979"*—dotted their once-peaceful meadow.

A hush fell over the crowd as the first ray streaked through the clear substance in the object on top of the pedestal. A rainbow of light cascaded over the milhooks, dressing them in brilliant colors that intensified as the suns climbed higher.

For minutes the milhooks stared at one another in wonder, seeing their neighbor, their friends, shining with colors they had never seen before. As the suns rose higher, the colors faded and the meadow returned to its ordinary shades of purple and blue. A gentle sigh escaped every milhook, from the oldest to the youngest. They all silently gave thanks to the heavens for sending them a rainbow.

THE EDITOR'S CORNER

At this time of year there is always much to be thankful for, not the least of which are the four terrific romances coming your way next month. These stories are full of warmth, passion, and love—just the thing for those cold winter nights. So make a date to snuggle up under a comforter and read the LOVESWEPTs we have in store for you. They're sure to heat up your reading hours with their witty and sensuous tales.

The wonderfully talented Terry Lawrence starts things off with a hero who's **A MAN'S MAN**, LOVESWEPT #718. From the moment Reilly helps Melissa Drummond into the helicopter, she is enthralled—mesmerized by this man of mystery who makes her feel safe and threatened all at once! Sensing the needs she's long denied, he tempts her to taste desire, to risk believing in a love that will last. Once he's warned her that he'll woo her until he's won, she must trust his promises enough to vow her own. This tale of irresistible courtship is another Terry Lawrence treasure.

THE COP AND THE MOTHER-TO-BE, LOVESWEPT #719, is the newest heartwarming romance from Charlotte Hughes. Jake Flannery had shared Sammie Webster's grief at losing her husband, cared for her as her child grew inside her, and flirted with her when she knew no one could find a puffy pregnant lady sexy—but she doesn't dare wonder why this tough cop's touch thrills her. And Jake tries not to imagine making love to the feisty mom or playing daddy to her daughter. But somehow their cherished friendship has turned to dangerous desire, and Jake must pull out all the stops to get Sammie to confess she'll adore him forever. The ever popular Charlotte Hughes offers a chance to laugh and cry and fall in love all over again.

Get ready for Lynne Bryant's **DAREDEVIL**, LOVESWEPT #720. Casey Boone is Dare King's buddy, his best friend, the only girl he's ever loved—but now that he might never walk again, Dare King struggles not to let her see his panic . . . or the pain he still feels three years after she left him at the altar! Casey has never stopped loving her proud warrior but fears losing him as she'd lost her dad. Now she must find the courage to heal Dare—body and soul—at last. In this touching and sizzling novel, Lynne Bryant explores the power of love, tested but enduring.

Linda Cajio wants you to meet an **IRRESISTIBLE STRANGER**, LOVESWEPT #721. Leslie Kloslosky doesn't believe her friend's premonition that she'll meet the perfect man on her vacation in

England—right up to the instant a tall, dark stranger enters the cramped elevator and lights a fire in her blood! Fascinated by the willowy brunette whose eyes turn dark sapphire when he kisses her, Mike Smith isn't about to let her go . . . but will he be clever enough to elude a pair of thieves hot on their trail? Linda Cajio weaves a treasured romantic fantasy you won't forget.

Happy reading!

With warmest wishes,

Beth de Guzman

Beth de Guzman

Senior Editor

P.S. Don't miss the women's novels coming your way in December: **ADAM'S FALL,** from blockbuster author Sandra Brown, is a deliciously sensual story of a woman torn between her duty and her heart; **PURE SIN,** from nationally bestselling author Susan Johnson, is a sensuous tale of thrilling seduction set in nineteenth-century Montana; **ON WINGS OF MAGIC,** by the award-winning Kay Hooper, is a classic contemporary romance of a woman who must make a choice between protecting her heart and surrendering to love once more. We'll be giving you a sneak peek at these wonderful books in next month's LOVESWEPTs. And immediately following this page look for a preview of the terrific romances from Bantam that are *available now!*

Don't miss these incomparable books
by your favorite Bantam authors

On sale in October

WANTED
by Patricia Potter

SCANDAL IN SILVER
by Sandra Chastain

THE WINDFLOWER
by Sharon and Tom Curtis

Winner of the *Romantic Times* 1992
Storyteller of the Year Award

PATRICIA POTTER

NATIONALLY BESTSELLING
AUTHOR OF *RELENTLESS*
AND *NOTORIOUS*

WANTED

*Texas Ranger Morgan Davis hadn't grown up with much
love, but he had been raised with respect for duty and the
law. To him, Lorilee Braden was nothing but a con artist,
yet her fire and beauty drew him despite his better judgment. Still, her brother was wanted for murder—and the
face on the wanted poster looked far too much like Morgan's for comfort. The only way he could clear his own
name was to bring Nicholas Braden to justice . . . before
the spark Lori had lit became a raging blaze that consumed
everything Morgan believed in . . .*

Braden balked at moving again. "Where's my sister?"

"In back," Morgan said. He led his prisoner to the
tree several yards behind the cabin. The woman immediately saw Nicholas Braden, her eyes resting on
the handcuffs for a moment, then she glared at Morgan.

Braden stepped over to his sister, stooped down,

and awkwardly pulled the gag from her mouth. "Are you all right?"

Morgan leaned back lazily against a tree and watched every movement, every exchange of silent message between the sister and brother. He felt a stab of longing, a regret that he'd never shared that kind of caring or communication with another human being.

Braden tried to untie his sister, but the handcuffs hindered him. Morgan heard a muffled curse and saw the woman's face tense with pain.

"Move away," Morgan said to Braden. Braden hesitated.

"Dammit, I'm not going to keep repeating myself." Irritation and impatience laced Morgan's words.

Braden stood, took a few steps away.

"Farther," Morgan ordered. "Unless you want her to stay there all night."

Braden backed up several feet, and Morgan knelt beside Lorilee Braden. With the knife from his belt, he quickly cut the strips of cloth binding her. Unfamiliar guilt rushed through him as he saw blood on her wrists. He hadn't tied her that tightly, but apparently the cloth had cut into her skin when she'd struggled to free herself.

His gaze met hers, and he was chilled by the contempt there. He put out his hand to help her up, but she refused it, trying to gain footing by herself. Her muscles must have stiffened because she started to fall.

Instinctively reaching out to help her, Morgan dropped the knife, and he saw her go for it. His foot slammed down on it. Then her hand went for the gun in Braden's gunbelt, which Morgan had slung over his shoulder.

Morgan swore as he spun her around, his hand going around her neck to subdue her. Out of the corner of his eye, he saw Nicholas Braden move toward him. "Don't," Morgan said. "I might just make a mistake and hurt her."

All rage and determination, she was quivering against him, defying him with every ounce of her being.

"You do real well against women, don't you?" Braden taunted.

Morgan had always had a temper—he felt ready to explode now—but his voice was even and cold when he spoke. "You'd better tell your sister to behave herself if she wants you to live beyond this day." His arms tightened around her. She wriggled to escape his hold, and he felt his body's reaction to it. It puzzled him. It infuriated him. He didn't like what he didn't understand, and he couldn't understand his reaction to this she-cat. She was trouble, pure trouble, but a part of him admired her, and he despised that admiration as a weakness in himself. "Tell her!"

"Lori."

Braden's voice was low but authoritative, and Morgan felt the girl relax slightly, then jerk away from him and run to her brother. Braden's handcuffed hands went over her head and around her, and he held her as she leaned trustingly against him. A criminal. A killer. A rare wave of loneliness swept over Morgan, flooding him with intense jealousy, nearly turning him inside out.

"Touching scene," he observed sarcastically, his voice rough as he tried to reestablish control—over his prisoner and the woman and over himself.

He tried to discipline his own body, to dismiss the

lingering flowery scent of Lorilee Braden, the remembered softness of her body against his. She was a hellion, he warned himself, not soft at all, except in body. He'd already underestimated her twice. He wouldn't do it again.

SCANDAL IN SILVER

BY

SANDRA CHASTAIN

"This delightful author has a tremendous talent that places her on a pinnacle reserved for special romance writers."—*Affaire de Coeur*

Sandra Chastain is a true reader favorite, and with SCANDAL IN SILVER, her new "Once Upon a Time Romance," she borrows from Seven Brides for Seven Brothers for a wonderfully funny and sensual historical romance about five sisters stranded in the Colorado wilderness with a silver mine.

"What was that?" he said, and came to a full stop.

To her credit she didn't jump up or cry out. Instead she looked around slowly, tilting her head to listen to the sounds of the night.

"I don't hear anything, Colter."

"We're being watched. Stand up slowly. Hold out your hand and smile."

She followed his directions, but the smiling was hard. She was certain there was nothing out there and that he knew it. This was a ruse. She'd known not to trust him; this proved it. "Now what?"

He returned her smile, dropped his wood and started toward her, speaking under his breath. "When I take your hand I'm going to put my arms around you and we'll walk deeper into the trees."

"Why?"

"I don't know what's going to happen, and I don't want to be out in the open." He hoped she didn't stop to examine that bit of inane logic.

"Shall I bring the rifle?"

"No, that would give us away."

He clasped her hand and pulled her close, sliding his arm around her as he turned her away from the fire. After an awkward moment she fitted herself against him and matched her steps to his.

"Is this good?" she asked, throwing her head back and widening her smile recklessly. The motion allowed her hat to fall behind her, freeing her hair and exposing her face to the light. She was rewarded by the astonished expression on his face. Two could play games, she decided.

His smile vanished. "Yes!" he said hoarsely. "You're getting the idea. In fact—"

"Don't you dare say I'm beautiful again, Captain Colter. Even a fool would know you are only trying to frighten me." She was looking up at him, her eyes stormy, her mouth soft and inviting. "Why?"

"I'm not trying to frighten you," he answered. She couldn't know how appealing she was, or that she was tempting him to kiss her. And he couldn't resist the temptation. He curled his arm, bringing her around in front of him as he lowered his head. His lips touched hers. She froze.

"Easy," he whispered, brushing his lips back and forth against a mouth now clamped shut. She gasped, parting her lips, and he thrust his tongue inside. Her jacket fell open as he pressed against her, almost dizzy from the feel of her. He felt her arm creep around him. For a long, senseless moment he forgot what he'd started out to do. The kiss that was meant to distract Sabrina had an unexpected effect on him.

Then she pulled back, returning them to reality. Her shock was followed by fear and finally anger. She slapped him, hard, with the palm of her healing hand.

Her eyes were wide. "What was all that about?" she asked as she backed away, one hand protectively across her chest, the other behind her.

"I don't know," he admitted ruefully, "but whatever it was, it's gone."

"I see. Then I don't suppose you'll need this now, will you?" She reached down and pulled the knife from her boot.

"No. I guess I won't."

"Concealing the knife in your bedroll was what this was about, wasn't it? Don't ever try something like that again, Captain Colter, or I'll use the knife on you."

She whirled around, and moments later she was inside the blanket, eyes closed, her entire body trembling like a snow rabbit caught in the gaze of a mountain lion.

She'd known there was nothing out there, but she'd let him play out his plan, wondering how far he'd go. She hadn't expected him to kiss her. But more than that she hadn't expected the blaze of fire that the kiss had ignited, the way her body had reached out, begging to be touched, the way her lips parted, inviting him inside.

"Guess you're not going to take the first watch," he finally said.

"You guessed right, soldier." Her throat was so tight that her words came out in a breathless rush.

"Got to you, did I?" he teased, surprising himself with the lightness of his tone. "The truth is, you got to me, too. But both of us know that nothing can come of it. No two people could ever be more un-suited to each other. It won't happen again."

"You're right, Colter. It won't. As for why I re-sponded, perhaps I have my own ways of distraction."

Her claim was brave, but he didn't believe she'd kissed him intentionally. He didn't even try to analyze the kiss. Giving thought to the combustion only fu-eled the flame. Best to put it behind them.

"Sweet dreams, madam jailer. I hope you don't have nightmares. I'm unarmed."

Sabrina didn't answer. He was wrong. He had a weapon, a new and powerful one against which she had no defense. He'd started a wildfire and Sabrina felt as if she were burning up.

THE WINDFLOWER

BY

SHARON AND TOM CURTIS

"Sharon and Tom's talent is immense."
—LaVyrle Spencer

With stories rich in passion and filled with humor, bestselling authors Sharon and Tom Curtis have become two of the most beloved romance novelists. Now this extraordinarily talented writing team offers a captivating tale of love and danger on the high seas, as a young woman is kidnapped and taken to an infamous privateering ship and her mysterious, golden-haired captor.

"You're very amusing, you know," he said.

For the first time since she'd left the tavern, she felt an emotion stirring within her that was not terror.

"I wasn't aware that I was being amusing," she said, a terse edge to her voice.

"I never supposed you were aware of it. But don't you think you were being a little overly conscientious? Under the circumstances."

Unfortunately his statement hit uncomfortably close to the truth. Before she could stop herself, Merry bit out, "I suppose *you* think nothing of knocking whole villages to the ground."

"Nothing at all," he said cheerfully.

"And terrorizing innocent women!" she said, a tremble in her voice.

"Yes. Innocent ones," he said, running his palm along her flat stomach, "and not so innocent ones."

She nearly fainted under his touch. "Don't do that," she said, her voice cracking in good earnest.

"Very well," he said, removing his hand. He went back to lean against the porch, resting on the heels of his hands, his long finely muscled legs stretched before him, and gave her an easy smile. "Don't run away from me, little one. For the moment you're much safer here."

Something in her face made him laugh again. "I can see you don't believe it," he continued. "But stay with me nevertheless. If you run off, I'll have to chase you, and I don't think we want to scamper across the beach like a pair of puppies."

She wondered if that meant he wouldn't invest much energy in trying to catch her if she did try to run and if it might not be worth the risk.

Reading her thoughts with alarming precision, he asked good-humoredly, "Do you think you could outrun me?"

It was hardly likely. A man used to safely negotiating the rigging during a high wind would be quick enough to catch her before she could even think of moving, and strong enough to make her very sorry. Involuntarily her gaze dropped to his hard legs, with their smooth, rhythmical blend of healthy muscle.

"Like what you see?" he asked her.

Merry's gaze flew to his, and she blushed and swallowed painfully. In a ludicrously apologetic voice she managed, "I beg your pardon."

"That's quite all right." He reached out his hand and stroked beneath her chin. "Much too conscientious. Would it surprise you to know, my little friend, that having you stare at my legs is the most uplifting thing that's happened to me all day?"

It was not the kind of remark she had remotely conceived a man might make to a woman, but there was something in his matter-of-fact delivery that made her suspect that he had participated in a great many conversations in precisely this style. Wishing she could match the ease of his tone, she said, "It's a pity your days are so dull."

"Oh, yes," he said with a glimmer of amusement, "in between knocking down villages and making people walk the plank, pirates really have very little to do."

Merry wondered briefly how she could ever have been so foolish as to have actually *wished* for an adventure.

"I don't know how you can talk about it like that," she said weakly.

He smiled. "I take it you don't usually flirt with villains."

"I don't flirt with *anyone*," Merry said, getting angry.

"I believe you don't, darling."

For a second his kind, enticing gaze studied her face, and then he looked away to the south, where a tiny flicker began to weave through the rocks. Another star of light appeared, and another, dragon's breath in the night.

"My cohorts," he observed. Offering her a hand, Devon inclined his head toward the dark-blue shadows that crept along the tavern's north side. "Come with me, I'm sure you don't want them to see you."

"*More* pirates?" said Merry hoarsely, watching the lights.

"Six more. Seven, if Reade is sober."

She hesitated, not daring to trust him, her face turned to him with the unconscious appeal of a lost child.

"Come with me," he repeated patiently. "Look at it this way. Better one dreadful pirate than seven. Whatever you're afraid I'll do to you, I can only do it once. *They* can do it seven times. Besides, I'm unarmed. You can frisk me if you want." His arm came around her back, drawing her away from the tavern. Grinning down at her, he said, "As a matter of fact, I wish you would frisk me."

She went with him, her footsteps as passive as a dreamer.

It seemed quite unnecessary to tell him. Nevertheless Merry said, "I've never met anyone like you in my life."

OFFICIAL RULES

To enter the sweepstakes below carefully follow all instructions found elsewhere in this offer.

The **Winners Classic** will award prizes with the following approximate maximum values: 1 Grand Prize: $26,500 (or $25,000 cash alternate); 1 First Prize: $3,000; 5 Second Prizes: $400 each; 35 Third Prizes: $100 each; 1,000 Fourth Prizes: $7.50 each. Total maximum retail value of Winners Classic Sweepstakes is $42,500. Some presentations of this sweepstakes may contain individual entry numbers corresponding to one or more of the aforementioned prize levels. To determine the Winners, individual entry numbers will first be compared with the winning numbers preselected by computer. For winning numbers not returned, prizes will be awarded in random drawings from among all eligible entries received. Prize choices may be offered at various levels. If a winner chooses an automobile prize, all license and registration fees, taxes, destination charges and, other expenses not offered herein are the responsibility of the winner. If a winner chooses a trip, travel must be complete within one year from the time the prize is awarded. Minors must be accompanied by an adult. Travel companion(s) must also sign release of liability. Trips are subject to space and departure availability. Certain black-out dates may apply.

The following applies to the sweepstakes named above:

No purchase necessary. You can also enter the sweepstakes by sending your name and address to: P.O. Box 508, Gibbstown, N.J. 08027. Mail each entry separately. Sweepstakes begins 6/1/93. Entries must be received by 12/30/94. Not responsible for lost, late, damaged, misdirected, illegible or postage due mail. Mechanically reproduced entries are not eligible. All entries become property of the sponsor and will not be returned.

Prize Selection/Validations: Selection of winners will be conducted no later than 5:00 PM on January 28, 1995, by an independent judging organization whose decisions are final. Random drawings will be held at 1211 Avenue of the Americas, New York, N.Y. 10036. Entrants need not be present to win. Odds of winning are determined by total number of entries received. Circulation of this sweepstakes is estimated not to exceed 200 million. All prizes are guaranteed to be awarded and delivered to winners. Winners will be notified by mail and may be required to complete an affidavit of eligibility and release of liability which must be returned within 14 days of date on notification or alternate winners will be selected in a random drawing. Any prize notification letter or any prize returned to a participating sponsor, Bantam Doubleday Dell Publishing Group, Inc., its participating divisions or subsidiaries, or the independent judging organization as undeliverable will be awarded to an alternate winner. Prizes are not transferable. No substitution for prizes except as offered or as may be necessary due to unavailability, in which case a prize of equal or greater value will be awarded. Prizes will be awarded approximately 90 days after the drawing. All taxes are the sole responsibility of the winners. Entry constitutes permission (except where prohibited by law) to use winners' names, hometowns, and likenesses for publicity purposes without further or other compensation. Prizes won by minors will be awarded in the name of parent or legal guardian.

Participation: Sweepstakes open to residents of the United States and Canada, except for the province of Quebec. Sweepstakes sponsored by Bantam Doubleday Dell Publishing Group, Inc., (BDD), 1540 Broadway, New York, NY 10036. Versions of this sweepstakes with different graphics and prize choices will be offered in conjunction with various solicitations or promotions by different subsidiaries and divisions of BDD. Where applicable, winners will have their choice of any prize offered at level won. Employees of BDD, its divisions, subsidiaries, advertising agencies, independent judging organization, and their immediate family members are not eligible.

Canadian residents, in order to win, must first correctly answer a time limited arithmetical skill testing question. Void in Puerto Rico, Quebec and wherever prohibited or restricted by law. Subject to all federal, state, local and provincial laws and regulations. For a list of major prize winners (available after 1/29/95): send a self-addressed, stamped envelope entirely separate from your entry to: Sweepstakes Winners, P.O. Box 517, Gibbstown, NJ 08027. Requests must be received by 12/30/94. DO NOT SEND ANY OTHER CORRESPONDENCE TO THIS P.O. BOX.